Best Friends' Bakery

Cupcakes & Contests

LINDA CHAPMAN

Illustrated by Kate Hindley

Orion
Children's Books

First published in Great Britain 2015
by Orion Children's Books
a division of the Orion Publishing Group Ltd
Orion House
5 Upper St Martin's Lane
London WC2 9EA
An Hachette UK company

1 3 5 7 9 10 8 6 4 2

Printed in Great Britain by Clays Ltd, St Ives plc

ISBN 978 1 4440 1192 0

www.orionbooks.co.uk

To Amany, who says the loveliest things,
and to Danny Jimminson for all the baking
and bread-making advice!

MY BAKING BOOK (and other stuff)

Name: Hannah

Age: $10^{7}/8$

Birthday: 1st August

Likes: baking, drawing, swimming, seeing my friends

Dislikes: spiders and slugs

This is my journal. It's for all sorts of important things - lists, cake designs, cookery facts, a few other things, but most of all for RECIPES!

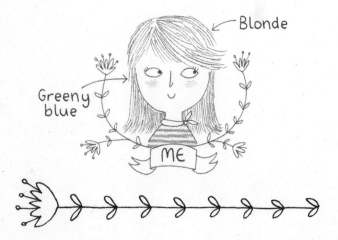

Blonde

Greeny blue

ME

1

I always think that if there's something you really want, you shouldn't wait for it to happen, you should MAKE it happen. My mum says, *A cake won't bake itself*. Just getting the ingredients together on a table isn't enough. You need to measure and mix and stir and bake.

It's like my mum. For years she's talked about running a bakery – and now she's actually made it happen. Five and a half weeks ago she opened the Sugar and Spice Bakery. It's officially my favourite place in the world.

SUGAR & SPICE
BAKERY
the BEST bakery
in the WORLD!

I really want my own bakery too when I'm older. My best friend, Mia, and I are going to open one and live in a flat above it. I definitely want to make that happen. There's something else I want to happen as well, something no one else knows about yet because I've only just found out about it. It's so exciting! But before I go into that, what else do you need to know about me?

My name's Hannah Hallett and I'm going to be eleven in a few months – on the first of August, to be precise. My mum and dad split up when I was a baby. My dad lives in America and I don't see him much, though we keep in touch by Skype and email.

Mum got married again a few months ago. I like Mark, my new stepdad. He's really

2

kind and makes Mum happy. He has twin daughters, Molly and Ella, who are four. Mark's first wife died, so the twins live with us, which means I'm now a big sister. It's strange not to be an only child any more but most of the time I like it – except when they wake me up super early. And it does mean that life is a LOT noisier at home.

After Mum and Mark got married, we moved to a town called Ashingham so Mum could open the bakery. I had to change schools and now I go to King William's middle school. I'd never heard of middle schools before we moved here. King William's has pupils in Years Five, Six, Seven and Eight. It feels much more grown up than my old primary school; more like a secondary school.

As well as Mia, I've made friends with Alice, Misha and Lara who are in my form. And that's about all you need to know, I think. Oh, apart from the thing I told you about – the thing I really, really want to make happen.

I've just been on the computer doing research on snow leopards for my homework, and I decided to take a quick look at the website of my all-time favourite TV show, *Junior Brilliant Baker* – and guess what? They're looking for people to audition for the next series of the show!

It would be the most awesome thing *ever* to be on JBB (that's what Mia and I call it). I can't wait till Mum comes home so I can ask her. I usually go to the bakery to help after school, but today I had too much homework. Ever since I saw they needed contestants for JBB I haven't been able to concentrate on my homework at all. Mum *has* to say yes – she just has to! This is one thing I am definitely going to MAKE happen!

REASONS I SHOULD BE ON JUNIOR BRILLIANT BAKER:

1. I am the show's biggest fan. I've watched every episode ever.
2. I can bake most things and I'm sure I wouldn't make the silly mistakes some contestants do, like forgetting to add sugar or burning my biscuits.
3. I'm good at coming up with recipes that are a bit different - Mia and I made some cookies at Baking Club at school and we changed the recipe and Miss Harris said the cookies tasted even nicer than they would have done with the original recipe.

Pierre Bertrand

Sandra Healey

Pierre Bertrand is Mum's favourite baker! He's French and he makes amazing pastry. Piercing blue eyes, quite wrinkly and a bit scary!

Sandra Healey is smiley, friendly, reminds me a bit of Mum. Has her own TV series and has written lots of books.

Please, please, PLEASE let Mum say yes!

2

As soon as I heard Mum's key in the front door I raced downstairs. "Mum!" I gasped. "You'll never guess ... Oh, you have to say I can do it – please, please, please!"

Mum put her bag on the floor. "Whoa! What's this? What do I have to say yes to?"

Before I could explain, Mark came through from the kitchen and gave Mum a kiss. "How was your day?"

"Rose!" squealed Molly, charging in from the lounge. She was wearing two tutus over her dress and a pair of sparkly fairy wings. She waved a wand made from a wooden spoon with tinsel stuck on. "Look at my magic wand! I made it all by myself!"

"And look at my picture of Super Dog fighting a pirate!" cried Ella, shoving a piece of paper into Mum's hands.

"Shall I give you a wish?" Molly asked. "You can have anything you want because I'm a fairy."

"Have you brought anything home for us?" asked Ella, peering into Mum's bag.

"Mum! I really need to talk to you about something," I said. "This is IMPORTANT!"

"Hey, girls," Mark said to Molly and Ella. "Why don't we give Hannah and Rose some time to chat? We could go to the park. Who wants to go on the swings and slide?"

"Me!" they cried.

"Get your shoes then," he told them, pulling on his coat.

I gave him a grateful look.

"Thanks," said Mum.

"No problem," Mark grinned. "This way, you two make dinner while I hang around at the swings."

8

I knew that, despite what he said, Mark was being nice. He always tries to make sure Mum and I have some time on our own when we need it. He reminds me of a farmhouse loaf: strong, comforting, reliable. Mum is different – she's kind and understanding, but she's also got a bit of a temper and a stubborn streak (like me). I think of her as a hot cross bun – a mixture of sugar and spice.

Sorry, I know that sounds weird. I always imagine everyone I know as a pastry or bread or cake. Mia is like sourdough bread – easily overlooked on first glance, but the nicest person in the world when you get to know her. Alice is an iced cupcake, pretty inside and out;

MISHA

Misha is a strawberry tart, big, bold and attention-grabbing; Lara is quieter with a hidden sweetness – a blueberry muffin.

As for me – well, I think I'm probably an Eccles

LARA

cake – not too special on the outside, but nice in the middle and with a sweet, sugary coating that most people like. At least, I hope most people like me!

As the door shut behind Molly, Ella and Mark, the house became blissfully quiet.

Mum breathed out a sigh. "Right, let me get a cup of tea and you can tell me what's so important."

We went through to the kitchen. I love our kitchen. It's got cream cupboards, a long pine table and French windows that open onto the garden and let in lots of light. When it's warm we have the windows open, and Mum keeps pots of herbs and flowers on the patio outside.

Mum put the kettle on and sat down. "Come on, then. Tell me all."

I crossed my fingers. "You know the TV programme, *Junior Brilliant Baker*?"

"Your favourite show of all time, you mean?" she said with a smile. "Yes."

I crossed my toes too, in case it helped. "Well, I saw on the show's website that

11

they're looking for contestants for their next series. There's an online form to fill in – you have to send it with a photo and answer some questions. If they like your application, you get to audition and maybe be one of the twelve people on the show. Please can I apply?" My words came out in a rush.

Mum looked thoughtful. "OK," she said.

"Really?"

"Let me have a look at the form first. But I don't see why not."

"I'll show you now! It's on the website." Mum's iPad was on the kitchen table. I quickly found the *Junior Brilliant Baker* site. Mum nodded as she scrolled through the questions and the information for parents.

"Loads of people are bound to apply," she said. "So don't get your hopes up too much. But nothing ventured, nothing gained. You'll have to be quick – it says here the closing date for applications is Wednesday."

I leaped up and spun round. I knew I was acting like one of the twins after they'd eaten too many sweets, but I was too excited to sit

still. A thought suddenly crossed my mind.
Mia!

"Do you think Mia's mum and dad will
let her apply too?" I pulled out my phone.
Having a phone of my own is one of the
best things about going to a middle school.
Everyone in Year Six at King William's has a
phone because most people walk
to school with their friends or
get the school bus. When
we moved, Mum agreed
to let me have one too. I
texted Mia.

> Check out the news section of the JBB
> website. NOW!!!!!!!

I waited impatiently for a reply. Mia
isn't one of those people who is constantly
checking her phone, and I like that about
her – I hate it if I'm with friends and they're
constantly texting other people – but
sometimes, like when I needed to get in
touch with her straightaway, it can be really
annoying!

I helped Mum get dinner ready. She'd brought a loaf back from the bakery and a few leftover lemon cupcakes. I arranged the cupcakes on a plate and put the bread on a wooden board on the table, breathing in its yummy smell. "Was there much left today?" I asked.

"Almost nothing," Mum said. "We pretty much sold out. I had to put this loaf aside or it would have gone too!"

I was pleased she'd been busy. The first week we'd opened, we'd had hardly any customers. Mum had been really worried, but then we'd printed some leaflets and taken them to the local farmers' market and word had spread. Now it seemed that every day was a busy day.

We chatted about the bakery as Mum heated up some homemade chicken soup and I set the table.

After a little while, we heard the door opening and Mark and the twins coming back. Alongside Mark's deep voice and the twins' high chatter, there was another male voice. One I didn't recognise. Mum and I gave each other a puzzled look. We both went to the kitchen door.

A tall man was standing with Mark. He had thick blond hair, broad shoulders and wore small round glasses. He was wearing cycling gear. I'm not very good at guessing the age of grown-ups but, if I had to, I'd say he looked about twenty-five.

"This is Stefan," Mark said. "He's just started at Graphite." Graphite was the company where Mark worked as a website designer. "We bumped into him in the park."

Stefan smiled. "Quite literally." I noticed he had a foreign accent.

"Ella was pretending to be Superdog and ran straight in front of his bike," Mark explained.

"I didn't get hurt," said Ella.

"Stefan did, though," said Molly. "He fell off."

15

"It was a sudden stop," admitted Stefan.

"Goodness, are you OK?" Mum asked.

Stefan smiled. "I am fine. Just a few grazes." He threw Ella a smile. "At least Superdog wasn't injured. She lives to fight another day."

"Superdog!" cried Ella, spreading her arms and running round the hall.

"Come through and have a drink," said Mum to Stefan, gesturing into the kitchen.

Stefan and Mark followed us. "Something smells good," said Stefan.

"Just soup. You're welcome to stay and have some with us if you like," offered Mum.

"Yes," said Mark. "Why don't you stay, Stefan?"

Stefan looked pleased. "Thank you. That's very kind of you. I'd love to."

I put out some more cutlery and a bowl and we all sat down. The twins came in for some cupcakes, then they went to watch TV in the lounge – they'd already eaten at their childminder's house.

"So, where did you work before Graphite, Stefan?" Mum asked.

"A company in Germany. I just moved to England two weeks ago."

"What brought you over here?" Mum asked.

"My grandparents on my father's side are English and I decided it would be a good experience to come and work here for a few years. Ashingham is a beautiful town. Mark tells me you have a bakery?"

"Yes. It's called the Sugar and Spice Bakery," Mum said.

Stefan smiled. "A good name. In baking you need both sugar and spice. In Germany we often use both in our pastries. Like Stollen at Christmas – soft bread and sweet raisins mixed with cardamom and cinnamon." He sighed. "I must make some this year. A taste of home."

"Do you like to bake, then?" I asked.

He nodded. "Very much." He held up a piece of Mum's bread. "May I say, this is delicious. I've never had bread quite like it."

"It's an old English type of bread called Sleepless White," Mum said.

"It's fermented overnight for sixteen hours," I added.

Mum nodded. "That's what gives it its flavour – it keeps for longer than normal bread too."

Mark shook his head at us. "I'm sorry, Stefan. There's no stopping Rose and Hannah when they start talking about baking."

Stefan smiled. "This is fine by me. Maybe we can swap some recipes. You show me how to make this English bread and I will show you how to make the German breads I love – pumpernickel, *Vollkornbrot* and *Roggenmischbrot*. Yes?"

"Definitely," Mum said.

"Oh, yes!" I said.

Mark grinned. "I'll go and get us some more drinks."

Mum, Stefan and I chatted about baking non-stop. It was really interesting hearing about the different breads and pastries they have in Germany. I couldn't wait to get my journal and write about them. Stefan told us he hadn't met many people in Ashingham yet apart from at work.

"You should join a club of some sort," Mark said, as Stefan got up to leave. "I think there's a cycling club in town."

"I will look into it," said Stefan. "Or maybe a running club. I like to run too."

"I'll have to come with you one day," said Mark.

"You're welcome here whenever you like," Mum said.

"And come and visit us in the bakery," I said.

"I will." Stefan put his head round the lounge door. Ella and Molly were snuggled under a big blanket.

"Goodnight, Superdog. Goodnight, little fairy."

"Bye, Stefan!" they called.

"What a nice guy," Mum said, as the door shut behind him.

19

"Isn't he?" said Mark. "It must be a bit lonely for him not knowing anyone."

"We'll have to have a baking day to swap recipes," I told Mum. "We could ask lots of people round and he'd get to know them."

She looked thoughtful. "Yes, I'm sure we could do something like that." She kissed my head. "Now, have you done all that homework?"

"Um ..." I thought of the endangered animals project that was unfinished because I'd been too busy thinking about *Junior Brilliant Baker* auditions. "Not quite."

"Then go and do it, please."

I sighed and headed for the stairs.

"Oh, and Hannah?"

"Yes?"

"When you've finished, maybe – just maybe – I'll come and have a look at the *Junior Brilliant Baker* form with you and fill in the parental consent details. Is that a deal?"

"It's a deal!" I called, springing up the stairs two at a time.

THINGS I'VE LEARNED
ABOUT GERMAN BAKING FROM STEFAN

I'm not sure what sort of bake
Stefan is yet - a type of bread maybe?
Granary? Farmhouse white?

· Germany has more
different types of
bread than any
country in the world -
almost a thousand.

· Bakeries in Germany usually have at
least twenty different kinds of bread
on sale at one time.

· Dark breads are more common than
white breads in Germany.

· Lots of German breads
have seeds and nuts
added, and are made
using rye.

- They have lots of different
cakes in Germany too
- big round ones made
from layers of dough
and filled with cream,
baked fruit, marzipan or
chocolate.

- At Christmas, they make Stollen - a
sweet dough with spices and dried
fruit in, a bit like a hot cross bun
but dusted with icing sugar. They
bake it in October/November and
then save it until December.

3

When I was getting ready for bed, Mum brought the iPad into my room with the audition form up on the screen. The form had the logo I knew so well at the top: Junior Brilliant Baker, written inside a mixing bowl. I put it on my desk. There were lots of questions to answer. Some were simple – like my name, address, date of birth – but there were some harder ones too. What did I like about baking? Who was my baking hero? How would I describe myself?

"Maybe you should think about it for a little while," Mum said, reading the questions over my shoulder. "I'll print you out a copy of the form so you can write your answers in rough first. You'll want to make it sound as good as possible."

I nodded. I definitely didn't want to mess it up.

She kissed me. "Night then, sweetheart. Lights off in ten minutes." As she left, my phone buzzed. It was Mia. Finally!

OMG! Only just saw ur txt. Auditions for JBB! Mum says I can send in the form. Did u ask ur mum yet?

I replied, She said yes!!!! Let's plan the forms 2gether.

OK. How amazing if we get on JBB!

I read her text and shut my eyes, imagining it with every brain cell I had. It would be awesome.

I texted back. We HAVE to! C u tmrw. x

Night ☺

I put my phone down and got into bed. I seriously couldn't wait until the next day!

Mia arrived at my house at half past eight next morning. Some days Alice joins us on the walk to school – her gran lives next door – but today it was just me and Mia.

I called goodbye to Mark and the twins. Mum was already at the bakery. She starts at five o'clock every morning. That's one of the few bad things about being a baker!

"Did you print out the form?" Mia said.

"Yes, it's in here," I replied, patting my bag.

"This is so exciting!" Mia said, her green eyes shining. "Do you really think we have a chance of getting on the show?"

"I don't know. Mum says there will be lots of people applying, but wouldn't it be amazing if we did?"

"It would be scary, but really good. Have you thought about your answers?" Mia asked.

"A bit, though I still don't have a clue what I'm going to say. How about you?"

We talked about it all the way to school. As we walked through the gates we saw

Miss Harris

Miss Harris parking her car. Miss Harris runs the Baking Club Mia and I go to on Thursday lunchtimes. She's quite young for a teacher and she's very smiley.

"Hi, girls!" she said, waving at us.

"Hi, Miss Harris," we chorused.

"You two look cheerful this morning," Miss Harris said.

"We are," I said. I pulled the JBB form out of my bag and showed it to her. "We're going to audition."

"How exciting!" Miss Harris said. "Good luck!"

"Thank you!" we said.

We found Misha, Alice and Lara by the lockers. Misha was telling the others about something. She was so busy with her story she didn't notice us approaching. She waved her arms in the air.

"So there she was in Sainsbury's, just taking a packet of pasta off the shelf, and she saw me

26

and *spoke* to me." Misha threw her hands in the air. "It was *soooo* embarrassing!"

"What's the drama? Who spoke to you?" I said, putting my bag down.

Misha turned. "Hi, Hannah. Hi, Mia. I was just telling the others about meeting Miss Harris in *Sainsbury's*!" Misha made it sound as if she'd met Miss Harris on the moon. "She said hello to me. I mean, embarrassing or what?"

I grinned. "Oh yeah, *really* embarrassing," I said. The others didn't seem to realise I was being sarcastic. They nodded.

"I hate it when you see teachers in shops," said Alice.

"It just feels wrong," agreed Lara.

I rolled my eyes. "That's dumb." Quite a lot of the teachers from school come into the bakery, so I'm used to seeing them doing normal things like shopping. "Where are they supposed to do their shopping if they don't go to shops?"

"They should just live in schools," said Misha. "And have food delivered."

I shook my head and carried on sorting my bag. My entry form for *Junior Brilliant Baker* fell out.

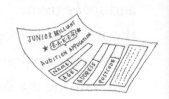

"What's this?" asked Alice, picking it up.

"Only the most exciting thing ever! Mia and I are going to apply to go on *Junior Brilliant Baker*."

Alice and Lara gasped and Misha squealed. "OMG! You're going to be on TV!"

"Well, not *definitely*," I said. "We've got to audition first."

"What have you got to do?" asked Alice.

Mia and I told them all about it. When the bell rang, Mia picked up her bag and went to her classroom. (Mia is in a different form to me, Misha, Alice and Lara.) "We'll talk more about our answers to the questions at break, OK?" I told her.

She beamed. "OK!"

Mia and I were still discussing the answers when we got to the bakery that afternoon. Mia's mum has a wedding dress shop nearby so Mia usually comes back with me. We're not old enough to work properly yet but we help behind the counter. We wrap the pastries and bread and chat to the customers while Paula, who works there full-time, takes the money. It's really fun because you get to know the regular customers.

"So, you're going to say that Mary Berry is your baking hero," I said to Mia as we opened the door. "And I'm going to say my mum is mine."

"Yeah," Mia agreed. "And you'll say you like making bread best and I'll say pastry."

"Hello, girls!" called Paula. She was polishing the counter top. Paula is small and round with dark hair and bright eyes. She's in her fifties and seems to know almost everyone in Ashingham. And, as she'll tell you, she's a Sagittarius. She's mad about horoscopes! "Could this conversation have anything to do with a certain bakery programme?" she asked.

I was surprised. "How do you know?"

"Your mum told me. Today is definitely the day for you to fill out the forms." Paula picked up a newspaper from behind the till. "Look." She pointed at the horoscopes page. "'Leo,'" she read, looking at me. "'*A rolling stone gathers no moss. Today is the day to set wheels in motion. All your dreams could come true!*' And Pisces ..." she said to Mia.

"Here we go. '*With Mercury rising, now is the time to strike. What you want is within your reach*'." She clapped her hands. "See? It's the perfect day to apply. After all, the stars ..."

"Never lie," Mia and I finished for her.

"Exactly," said Paula. "So, best get to work!"

"We will," I promised.

The doorbell tinkled as a lady with a toddler came in. Mia and I went to leave our bags in the staffroom and wash our hands. We said a quick hello to Mum and her apprentice, Dylan, who were busy in the kitchen, and hurried out to help.

There was a flurry of customers coming to buy things for tea. For the next twenty minutes, Mia and I were too busy to chat. Then the rush eased and we were able to have a break. I was starving. Mum always lets us choose a treat to keep us going until dinner so we helped ourselves – I had a jam doughnut dusted with sugar and Mia had a squidgy chocolate brownie.

We had just finished when the door opened and Miss Harris came in. "Hi, Hannah. Hi, Mia."

"Hi, Miss Harris," we said.

She went to the counter. "I thought I'd pop in and get something for after my supper. What do you recommend?"

"The cupcakes are really good," I said.

"Or how about a brownie?" said Mia. "I've just had one and they're delicious."

"Or a chocolate éclair," Paula put in.

"Oh yes, an éclair sounds just the thing," said Miss Harris. "Could I take one of those, please?"

I started wrapping one up for her.

"How's work going, Jane?" Paula asked. "Are you still enjoying it?"

"Definitely," said Miss Harris. "Although I had no idea it was going to be so full on. I mean, the training was tough, but I thought it might be easier once I started school."

"Is this your first year as a teacher?" I asked.

She nodded. "My first job. I moved to Ashingham because of it."

"The workload will get easier, I'm sure," said Paula. "And it'll be the summer holidays before you know it."

"I know. I'm looking forward to being able to get out and meet more people," said Miss Harris. "I've been so busy working I haven't had a chance. I go jogging in the park but that's not very sociable."

"You should come to my belly-dancing classes," said Paula. "You'll meet lots of people and it's good exercise too." She put her arms above her head and did a little shimmy. "Tempted?"

"Maybe," said Miss Harris.

I shot a look at Mia. Miss Harris must be seriously desperate to meet people if she would consider belly dancing.

Paula took Miss Harris's money. "Well, belly dancing's on Thursday evenings. Just let me know whenever you fancy it."

"I will. Thanks, Paula," said Miss Harris. "Bye, girls, see you at school."

"Bye," we said.

We watched her leave.

"She sounds a bit lonely," Mia said.

"I think she is," said Paula. "She told me she doesn't have a boyfriend or partner, and it must be hard for her to make friends when she's so busy with work."

"That's what Stefan said too," I agreed. I told them about how nice our dinner guest last night had been. I still hadn't worked out what kind of bake he was. Miss Harris, though, was a mini-sized pain au chocolat – small, neat, sensible on the outside but with a sweet centre.

Suddenly I frowned. Stefan. Miss Harris. Two people who were new to Ashingham, two people who wanted to meet others.

I gasped. "Hey! I know how we can stop Miss Harris feeling lonely!"

4

"You're saying we should try and be matchmakers?" said Mia. "That we should get Miss Harris and this man, Stefan, together?"

"Yep," I said. "It would be perfect. They both enjoy baking and doing outside stuff like cycling and jogging. They're bound to get on."

"It's a wonderful idea!" said Paula.

"But how do we do it?" asked Mia, looking less certain.

"I guess we just have to try and arrange a meeting." I imagined Miss Harris and Stefan becoming boyfriend and girlfriend. Maybe they'd even get married! Mia and I could be bridesmaids and Mum could make the cake for the wedding and—

My daydream was interrupted by Dylan poking his head out of the kitchen.

DYLAN = a breadstick. Tall, thin. But not a plain breadstick. He's not boring at all. Maybe he'd be cheddar and chilli? Parmesan and paprika? Sun-dried tomato and olive?

DYLAN

"Hey, Skippy. Hey, Minnie!" Dylan calls me Skippy because I remind him of a bouncy kangaroo in some old kids' TV show he used to watch. Mia is Minnie after Minnie Mouse because Dylan says she's like a cute little mouse.

"Hi, Dylan," we said.

"You three look as if you're plotting something," he said.

"Maybe we are," said Paula, tapping the side of her nose.

"Tell me," said Dylan.

"No," I said. Dylan is so chatty, I had a feeling he would give the game away if he saw Miss Harris in the shop. "It's girl stuff."

"I can pretend to be a girl," Dylan said. He put on a high-pitched voice. "OMG, Hannah! That guy in the newsagents said hi. He must be totally into me! And have you seen my new shoes?" He pointed to his trainers.

I giggled. "Still not going to tell you."

He frowned. "Has anyone ever told you that you're really mean?"

The door opened and more customers came in. Mia and I hurried to wash our hands so we could help. After that, we were busy until closing time. As we said goodbye, Mia and I agreed to fill in our forms and email them in the morning. I also intended to do some serious thinking about exactly HOW we could get Miss Harris and Stefan together.

On the way home, Mum mentioned she was thinking of holding a bread-making workshop, because a few customers had asked about it.

"We couldn't have too many people because the kitchen isn't big enough, but we could probably fit around ten or so. I think it would be really fun. We could try an experimental one first – invite a few friends – and then, if it works, I'll hold another one and charge people for it."

I almost gasped out loud. This would be just the place for Stefan and Miss Harris to meet!

"I thought you and Mia could come, and Paula and Dylan, George and Sarah and Stefan," Mum went on.

"Could we invite Miss Harris too?" I asked.

Mum nodded. "Yes, of course. I thought I might run it next Saturday, after the bakery closes."

I texted Mia to tell her. It would be perfect for our matchmaking plans! I sighed happily. Now that was sorted, I could concentrate on the JBB form.

I wrote out the difficult answers.

What Do I Like About Baking?

Everything! I love putting something in the oven and having it come out totally different - it's like magic. I love the tastes, the smells, the feel of dough. I love seeing people eat my food and enjoy it.

Who is My Baking Hero?

My mum is my baking hero. She owns a bakery and everything she makes tastes delicious. She's taught me to try out different flavours and not to be afraid to make changes to a recipe.

How Would I Describe Myself?

Friendly, cheerful, determined, baking-mad.

When I was happy with what I'd written, I borrowed Mum's iPad and filled out the form. I was so engrossed that I didn't hear her calling me until she actually came upstairs. "Hannah? What are you doing? Dinner's ready."

"Sorry, I was doing this." I showed her the form.

Mum's eyes scrolled down it, then she smiled. "This is great, sweetheart. Maybe you will get an audition after all."

I glowed. "Do you really think so?"

"Well, I've no idea what they'll be looking for," she said. "But I think you stand a really good chance. Anyway, come and eat."

Before I went downstairs, I texted Mia:

I've almost finished my form. How about u?

For once, her reply pinged straight back.

Me too! Shall we send them off tonight?

YES! ☺ ☺ ☺

I put my phone in my pocket and hugged myself. Soon, our forms would be on their way – and someone, somewhere would make the decision. A thought struck me. What if Mia got asked to audition and I didn't? My tummy flipped over. *Oh, please let BOTH of us get chosen*, I wished, as I joined Mum, Mark and the twins at the table.

5

After sending off my application form, I pestered Mum to check her emails every day. I also checked the post the second I got home from school, just in case there was a letter from the JBB production company. But the days went by and there was no news.

"Have you heard anything yet, Skippy?" Dylan asked me, when Mia and I arrived at the bakery after school the following Friday.

"Not yet," I sighed.

"Maybe we'll hear tomorrow," said Mia hopefully.

"Maybe," said Dylan. "Although they might only contact the people they want to audition."

"Don't say that!" I said. I couldn't bear the thought of waiting and never finding out. I think that would be worse than getting a letter that just said no.

"Oh yeah, before I forget," said Dylan, picking up a brown paper bag, "Stefan left this for you." Stefan had started calling in at the bakery regularly, and if he was there in the afternoons he'd often stop and chat to me and Mia. I looked in the bag. Inside there was a small rectangular dark brown loaf.

"It's pumpernickel bread," Dylan explained. "He said he baked it so you could try some traditional German bread before the workshop tomorrow."

"Oh, cool!" I said. I tore a piece off. The bread hardly had any crust and was very dense and moist, with a sweet, malty smell. I offered the bag to Dylan and Mia so they could try some too.

"This is good. Stefan can certainly bake," said Dylan.

The bread had a sweet, earthy flavour, almost like dark chocolate. "This is it!" I said suddenly. "This is what Stefan is. I've been trying to work it out. He's a loaf of pumpernickel bread – strong, interesting, a bit sweet."

Dylan looked at me as if he thought I was nuts. "What are you talking about?"

I blushed bright red. "Oh … um … nothing."

Mia grinned. I'd told her how I liked to imagine people as different kinds of bakes, but I didn't usually didn't tell anyone else. "So, Stefan's definitely coming?" she said, changing the subject.

"Yes. He's looking forward to it."

My heart gave a little happy skip. We'd asked Miss Harris about it at school and she had said she would love to come. Tomorrow afternoon my matchmaking plan would begin!

Mia stayed at mine that
night. After dinner, we
made chocolate cupcakes.
I've been experimenting
making them with
olive oil instead of butter
recently. Mum had made
some olive oil, lemon and thyme
cupcakes for the bakery – she said that with
olive oil they were healthier and would
taste just as nice. Since then I've been trying
to work on the perfect olive oil chocolate
cupcake.

The first time I tried it, the cakes were
light and moist but not rich and chocolatey
enough, so I tried again with more cocoa
powder and using brown sugar instead of
white. That helped, though I still thought
they could be better. Today I was going to
frost them with chocolate ganache instead
of buttercream. A chocolate ganache is
just chocolate and cream, so it tastes really
chocolatey. I hoped it would be just what the
cupcakes needed.

45

"So, tomorrow," I said to Mia, as we piped ganache onto the cupcakes, "we need to make sure Stefan and Miss Harris start talking."

"Can't we just let them meet and get on with it?" said Mia.

"No, no, no," I told her. "A cake won't bake itself. We have to do some mixing and stirring."

"What do you mean?" Mia asked.

"Well, Mum says she's going to make everyone partner up, so we need to make sure they go together."

"How?" said Mia.

I'd already thought about this. "Easy. You

46

say you'll go with Miss Harris, and I'll say I'll go with Stefan and then we ask if we can swap – they'll have to be partners then!"

"OK," said Mia, nodding.

"Their eyes will meet across the work bench and they'll fall in love instantly," I said. "Neither of them will ever be lonely again. Love will be in the air, I bet you."

"I think it's in the air now. I'm in love with these cupcakes," Mia said. She picked one up and spoke to it solemnly. "Cupcake, you will never be lonely again!"

I picked up another. "Marry me, cupcake!"

We giggled and peeled back the cupcake cases. I took an enormous bite of mine. It was delicious. The ganache frosting had an intense chocolate flavour and the olive oil made the sponge light and delicious. The combination was amazing. "Mm-mm-mmm," I said.

"Mmm," Mia said.

I love baking, but the eating is even better!

CHOCOLATE AND OLIVE OIL CUPCAKES

Ingredients:

150g self-raising flour

50g plain flour

50g light brown sugar

150g caster sugar

50g unsweetened cocoa powder

½ teaspoon salt

3 medium eggs at room temperature

160ml light olive oil

60ml milk

½ teaspoon vanilla extract

What To Do:

1. Preheat oven to 180°C.

2. Line a 12-cup muffin tin
   with paper cases.

3. Mix the flour, cocoa and
   salt in a bowl.

4. In another bowl, use an
   electric whisk to beat eggs and
   sugar until creamy, then whisk in vanilla
   extract.

5. Gradually stir the flour, cocoa powder

and salt mixture into the egg and sugar mixture until combined. It will be very thick and hard to mix.

6. Slowly pour in the milk and then the olive oil, folding and stirring. Now the mixture should be shiny and glossy.

7. Spoon into your cake cases until they are about two-thirds full, and bake for 15-20 minutes until the centre of each cake is springy to the touch. If you turn the tray round halfway through baking, it will help the cupcakes bake evenly.

Quick Chocolate Ganache for Frosting

Ingredients:

250g chocolate, chopped into small pieces

230ml double cream

(You can use dark or milk chocolate. Dark chocolate gives a very intense taste. Milk chocolate makes a sweeter topping. Milk chocolate ganache doesn't whip so well so if I'm using it, I usually just spoon it on top.)

What To Do:

Place the chocolate pieces in
a bowl.
Heat cream in a pan on
a medium heat until it
just starts to bubble, then
pour the cream over the chocolate and mix
together. The chocolate will melt and the
mixture will become smooth and glossy. Either
spoon it onto the cakes or let it cool and
then whip it and pipe or swirl it onto the
cakes.

EAT AND ENJOY!!

6

On Saturday when the sign on the bakery
door had been turned to "closed", the
counters had been wiped and the cash till
emptied, everyone started to arrive for Mum's
bread-making workshop.

Stefan was first. "What did you think of the
pumpernickel bread?" he asked, shrugging
off his coat. "It was good?"

I couldn't resist teasing him. "No, Stefan, it
wasn't good," I said.

He gave me a hurt look.

I grinned. "It was A-MA-ZING!"

Stefan's face broke into a broad smile. "I
thought you were serious. I was worried."

"Sorry. It was awesome. Can
you teach me how to
make it?" I asked.

"It would be my
pleasure."

Just then Miss Harris
arrived.

"Oh look, that's my teacher, Miss
Harris. She runs our school Baking Club. I'd
better go and say hello. Why don't you come
with me?"

Stefan followed me, but as we crossed the
room Dylan came over. "Hey, Stefan! That
pumpernickel was excellent!"

"Ah, thank you. The trick is to bake it for
a long time with much steam." Stefan stopped
to chat to Dylan.

Aargh! I felt like stamping my foot in
frustration. But I reminded myself there was
the whole of the workshop to go, so there
was plenty of time for Miss Harris and Stefan
to get to know each other.

Just then my friend, George and his mum,
Sarah, arrived. George doesn't go to my

school – we met a few weeks ago when Sarah asked Mum to make a cake for him.

"Hi, Hannah," Sarah said. "This is exciting. I've never baked bread before."

"It'll be fun," I told her. "Mum says we're doing it the old-fashioned way without using a mixer. How is the beauty shop going?"

Sarah has just taken out a lease on a shop up the road from the bakery. She's going to sell natural hair and body beauty products that she makes herself. "Great! The decorators are busy getting ready and I've been experimenting with lots of different products at home."

"Our house stinks!" said George gloomily. "There are flowers and smelly oils everywhere."

"Boys," said Sarah, shaking her head. "He doesn't get it. You'll have to come and test some of the products for me."

"OK," I said. "I bet some of my friends would love to try them too." I looked slyly at George. "And George could join in. I think he'd look great with a face mask."

George's expression of horror made Sarah and me giggle.

Mum came out from the kitchen and clapped her hands. "Hello, everyone!" she said. "Thank you for coming to be my guinea pigs today. Come through and we can get started. Everyone, find a partner."

This was it! Time to put our plan into action!

"See you in a minute," I said to Sarah and George.

"Wait, Hannah!" said George, grabbing my arm. "Will you be my partner?"

"Umm ..."

"Please, I don't want to go with my mum! No offence, Mum," he said.

"None taken," Sarah said. "I'm sure you'll have more fun with Hannah than with me."

Ahead, Dylan and Stefan were heading to

the kitchen together. My heart sank. It looked as though they'd decided to be partners. So much for pairing Stefan up with Miss Harris.

I turned to George. "OK, I'll be your partner. Let's get into the kitchen." If they weren't partners, I wanted to at least make sure Stefan and Miss Harris were standing next to each other. "Come on!"

The huge wooden baker's bench in the kitchen was set with four workstations along one of the long sides. Each station had a jug of warm water, a baker's wheel for cutting the dough and pots filled with seeds and fresh herbs and flakes of sea salt. In the centre of the table, there was a huge mountain of flour, a block of yeast and a box filled with salt.

Dylan and Stefan stood at the far end of the bench.

I hurried over to stand next to them, and Mia and Miss Harris stood on our other side. Mia shot me a *what-happened?* look. I couldn't say anything to her but my mind was already whirring.

I smiled at Miss Harris. "Would you mind if George and I swapped places with you, Miss Harris?"

Miss Harris smiled. "Of course not; that's fine."

Annoyingly, George shook his head. "If we do that, I'll be next to Mum. Can't we stay here?"

"Yeah, stay here. This is the boys' end of the table," said Dylan.

I felt like kicking Dylan. Maybe I *should* have told him about the matchmaking plan after all!

"Right, everyone. Roll up your sleeves, remove any jewellery and wash your hands," Mum said. "It's time to get baking!"

Mum explained that we would begin with a traditional white dough and bake some different-flavoured breadsticks and bread rolls.

"Once we've made the dough, we'll divide it in two. The dough for the rolls will need to prove in a warm place for at least an hour before we can shape it but while that's happening we can make the breadsticks. There will be some waiting around, I'm afraid, once the breadsticks are in the oven, and I'll use that time to talk you through the science behind bread-making and give you a chance to taste a few different breads. For now – let's get mixing!"

Mum cut the block of yeast into chunks and gave a piece to each pair. We had to put it into the jug of warm water and rub it between our fingers until it dissolved and the water went cloudy. Mum explained that meant the yeast was activated and ready to use. We added a spoonful of honey and stirred it well. Then we had to make a well of flour in front of us, before pouring in the yeast, water and honey mix. After that it was time to get sticky!

Our hands and lower arms were soon covered. It was really good fun, even though George kept threatening to attack me with doughy hands! When I've made dough with Mum before we've always used a mixer, either the little one at home or the big dough brake in the bakery. It was really cool to watch the dough gradually change from a sloppy, sticky mess to a soft squidgy ball you could stretch and pull.

As I kneaded, I looked to my left and then to my right. Stefan and Miss Harris were both concentrating hard. Was now the time to try and get them talking?

"Have you been out in the park cycling again, Stefan?" I asked loudly, hoping that Miss Harris could hear on my other side.

"Most days," he said. "I either cycle or go for a run."

"Oh, wow!" I said, raising my voice even more. "Running in the park – that must be awesome!"

"You like running?" Stefan said.

I glanced over my shoulder. Was Miss Harris going to join in?

But she wasn't even listening. She was talking to Paula and Sarah.

"You could come running with me and Mark one day, if you like?" said Stefan.

I changed the subject hastily. "I think my dough's almost done." I pulled a ball off and stretched it out. When the dough is ready you should be able to stretch it out so that it becomes as thin as a sheet of paper and doesn't break. "How's yours, Stefan?"

"It's just about there," he said.

Mum told us to divide the dough using one of the baker's wheels. We put the dough for the rolls in one bowl and left that on the proving rack beside the oven. The breadstick dough went in another bowl to prove for fifteen minutes and, while we were waiting for it, we helped clean up.

Soon we were ready to start. "Your breadsticks don't have to be perfectly smooth and even," Mum told us. "So you don't need a rolling pin, just your hands. You can twist

them too." She showed us what she
meant. "Then add salt and pepper and
herbs – rosemary works well, as does
basil."

As we set to work, I tried to think
of another way to get Stefan and Miss
Harris talking.

Miss Harris had just finished laying out
her breadsticks on a baking tray. She picked
them up to carry them over to the proving
rack by the oven where they needed to prove
for another short while before going in the
oven. Pretending I needed the salt box, I
moved along the bench next to Stefan. As
Miss Harris passed us, I stumbled into
Stefan. He stepped back and bumped into
Miss Harris. It wasn't a big bump, and
I'd thought he would just apologise and
they would start chatting and realise how
much they had in common. Unfortunately,
Stefan was holding his jug of water. As he
bumped into her, his arm jolted and water
splashed out, covering Miss Harris and her
breadsticks.

She gasped in shock.

Stefan was horrified. "Oh no, I am so sorry."

"It's ... it's OK," said Miss Harris, flustered.

Stefan picked up a tea towel and tried to dab at her wet arms. But the tea towel had flour on it and it left white streaks wherever it touched.

Miss Harris jumped back. "Stop! You're making it worse!"

She looked down at her tray. "My breadsticks are ruined."

"It was my fault," I said. "I bumped into Stefan."

"Hannah, you have to be more careful," Mum said. She took the tray of breadsticks from Miss Harris. "I'm sorry about that, Jane. Look, I've got some spare dough. You can make some more breadsticks and I'll get you a clean cloth to get the flour off."

"Thank you," said Miss Harris, as Mum led her away.

"Whoops," muttered Stefan, raising his eyebrows at me.

"Whoops," I replied. So much for getting them talking.

"Maybe I should offer to help her make more breadsticks," said Stefan.

"That's a good idea," I said. But when he asked, Miss Harris shook her head. "I'm fine, thanks," she said, turning away.

Stefan went back to his bench. My heart sank. Matchmaking was definitely harder than it sounded.

I finished my own breadsticks, which I had flavoured with rosemary and coated with poppy seeds, and twisted them into a swirly stick shape. I showed them to Stefan before I put them on the proving rack. "What do you think?"

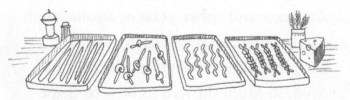

"They're not good," Stefan said seriously, just as Miss Harris was passing.

She frowned at him in surprise and carried on.

Stefan grinned. "They are A-MA-ZING!" he finished.

I glanced at Miss Harris but she was out of earshot. She must have thought Stefan was being really rude. Judging by the disapproving look she threw at him when she next passed, I was sure I was right. I groaned inwardly. Things were going from bad to worse.

While the breadsticks were in the oven, Mum explained different baking techniques and gave us some different breads to taste. We tried sourdough, which was soft on the inside with a crunchy crust, and rye bread, which had a malty flavour, as well as rosemary focaccia, pitta and some olive ciabatta. It's amazing that the same basic ingredients – flour, water and either yeast or a sourdough starter – can make such different breads!

By this time, the dough for the rolls had proved, so Mum showed us how to shape them into knots and batons and simple rounds. We added our own choice of seeds and finished them by brushing on an egg glaze. Then they went in the oven.

BREADSTICK FLAVOURS

Chilli and cheddar
Garlic and parmesan
Poppy seed and rosemary
Stilton and olive

ROLLS

By the end, the bench was filled with all the
rolls and breadsticks we had made. They
looked incredible – and the smell in the
kitchen was even better.

Mum took a photo for the bakery website
and then we packed everything into paper
bags to take home.

"So, maybe you will come running with me one day, Hannah?" Stefan said, as everyone was leaving.

"Um, maybe," I said.

Mia squealed. Everyone turned. She went as red as a tomato when she realised everyone was staring at her.

"What's the matter?" I said to her. It's almost unknown for Mia to make herself the centre of attention. "Are you OK?"

She held up her phone. "I've just had a text from Mum," she whispered. A strange expression crossed her face – a mixture of excitement and worry – as her eyes met mine. "Um ... a producer from *Junior Brilliant Baker* just rang and said they want me to go for an audition."

My heart leaped. That was brilliant! Then I felt a rushing, falling feeling and a horrible part of me thought, *What about me?*

There was only one thing to do, though. I put a big smile on my face.

"That's great, Mia! Well done! That's awesome!"

66

I felt Mum's arm around my shoulders. "Mia's not the only one," she said softly.

I caught my breath. "What do you mean?"

"Mark's just texted. We've had a phone call too. The audition is in two weeks' time."

The world seemed to spin. I opened and shut my mouth but no sound came out. Mia squealed again and ran over and grabbed my hands. "We're going to the auditions together, Hannah!" she said, jumping up and down.

Suddenly everyone was talking at once, hugging and congratulating us.

"We're going to the auditions!" I cried, spinning Mia round. "We're going to the JBB auditions!"

7

I was desperate to quiz Mark about what the producer had said. As soon as Mum and I got home I ran to find him.

"Calm down, calm down," he said, laughing. "They wanted to check if you were free to go to Nottingham and make sure we were OK with you being part of it. They're going to email your mum with the details."

Mum and I checked her email. There it was! An email from the production company with the heading 'Junior Brilliant Baker – Nottingham Auditions'. Seeing it in black and white made it suddenly seem very real.

The email said the production company was auditioning all around the country over the next couple of weekends and the Nottingham auditions  – my auditions – would be at the end of half term week. I had to take a sweet and a savoury bake and be prepared to talk about why I had chosen them and how I had made them. After everyone had been interviewed and their food tasted, a shortlist would be drawn up. The people on the shortlist would be asked to stay on for a screen test.

The email said that a lot of people had applied and only twelve would be chosen to go on the show.

"It's great you've been asked to audition, but try not to get your hopes up," Mum said, as she finished reading.

"I won't," I said, though I was hardly listening. One sweet thing and one savoury. How was I ever going to choose?

WHAT SHOULD I BAKE?

SAVOURY IDEAS

Bread, but what type?

Rolls - too simple?

Mum's sourdough bread - maybe.

Walnut and raisin?

Potato and rosemary?

German bread - pumpernickel?
TALK TO STEFAN!

SWEET

Birthday cake?

Cookies?

Chocolate brownies?

Olive oil and chocolate cupcakes?

GOT TO BE DIFFERENT
AND STAND OUT!

Next morning was Sunday and Mia came over. "I thought I might ask Dylan to show me how to make one of those meat pies he makes for the bakery," she said. "I was thinking I could do one with an unusual filling, like venison and cranberry or venison and sour cherry."

I felt a flash of envy. It was a great idea. I was sure the judges would be impressed.

"You're frowning. Don't you think it's any good?" Mia asked.

"No, it's great," I admitted. "I just wish that *I'd* thought of it. Listen, can we promise we won't let the show get in the way of our friendship?" I could feel myself blushing, I felt stupid even saying it, really. But Mia looked relieved.

"Definitely!" she said. "We stay best friends, no matter what."

We both smiled and I felt much happier. "You should do the venison pie," I said. "What about your sweet bake?"

"I thought I might do a chocolate brownie with ginger and macadamia nuts."

"Yum!" I said. "I was thinking of doing my olive oil cupcakes with the chocolate ganache. What do you think?"

Mia nodded. "They're the best cupcakes ever! What about your savoury?"

"Some sort of bread, I think. Maybe I could ask Stefan if he'll teach me how to make pumpernickel or another German bread."

"That's a good idea," said Mia. "That'll make you stand out."

I grinned. "Hopefully because the bread's good, not because it's rubbish."

"We have got a whole load of practising to do!" Mia said.

I tingled with excitement. This was going to be *so* much fun!

Mia and I spent the morning baking brownies and cupcakes. Mark, Mum and the twins were on tasting duty and told us what they thought after each batch so that we could make them even better. I still thought my

cupcakes needed
some extra
decoration or a
splash of colour.
Maybe paste
flowers to go on
top? I wandered to
the French windows and

went out to the patio. Bees and butterflies
were flying around the herbs and flowers
in the pots. There were some pretty purple
flowers that would be the perfect colour
for topping my cupcakes. I knew Mum
sometimes crystallised real flowers. Could I
do that with these? I picked a few and went
back inside.

Mum told me they were called violas and
that they would be fine to crystallise. She
showed us how to brush the flowers all over
with egg white and then sprinkle them with
caster sugar.

"Can you crystallise all flowers?" Mia
asked.

"You can, but you need to be careful and

always check with me or another adult to make sure you haven't chosen a flower that might be poisonous or cause an allergic reaction. The safest flowers are violas, like these, roses or nasturtiums," Mum told us.

"What do we do with them now?" I asked.

"We leave them in a warm place to dry and set for an hour or so. Then they'll be hard, and perfect for decorating."

"They're going to look beautiful!" Mia said.

I smiled. They were exactly the finishing touch I had been hoping for. "Now I just need to think about my savoury bake. I'm going to call Stefan and see if he'll show me how to bake pumpernickel."

"Just think, this time in two weeks we'll know if we're on the shortlist or not," Mia said.

I felt my tummy turn over. These two bakes were going to be the most important ones of our lives!

The two weeks seemed to creep by. Mia and I spent every spare minute practising. Luckily, Alice, Misha and Lara were as excited as we were about us auditioning for a TV show and they put up with all our baking talk.

Stefan showed me how to do his version of a German bread called *Vollkornbrot*, which is a little bit like pumpernickel but doesn't take as long to make. I hadn't realised that pumpernickel needed sixteen to twenty-four hours in the oven and then to rest for a couple of days before you eat it. *Vollkornbrot* is a dense, moist rye bread with a chewy crust. Stefan said he liked to add dried fruit, seeds and nuts to make it extra special. We baked two loaves to start with, one with added fruit, seeds and nuts and one without, so I could see the difference.

I practised making it lots over the next two weeks, experimenting with the mix of fruit, seeds and nuts. I would have to make the loaf for the competition on Thursday because, unlike fresh white bread, which is best eaten as soon as it's baked, rye bread tastes better if you leave it for a few days. It's to do with the flavour needing time to develop, Stefan says.

The night before the auditions, I set my alarm clock for 5.30 a.m. – I had to get up early to make my cupcakes.

I turned my light out and pulled my duvet around me. My mind was racing and I lay awake for a long time, wondering what the next day would hold.

Crystallised violas

Could use small mint leaves instead and flavour fanache with mint for mint chocolate cupcakes. Yum! Or try flavouring with orange essence.

8

The next morning, Mum drove to Mia's house to pick up Mia and her mum, Nicky. Mia and I exchanged anxious smiles as she climbed onto the back seat. We hardly said a word during the drive to Nottingham. I could tell she was as nervous as I was.

"Hannah Hallett and Mia Evans?" the lady from the production company said, checking her clipboard. She ticked off our names and gave us badges to wear. "Can you stick these on for me, girls? I'm Emily, by the way, one of the production assistants. If you need anything, just ask me."

I gazed around at the people arriving with their parents. I couldn't believe we were actually here! Mia squeezed my arm. *Today will go well, it will*, I told myself.

"Where do we go now?" Mia's mum asked Emily.

Emily pointed to a set of double doors. "If you head into that room, someone will show you where to set up your bakes. We'll be judging in about thirty minutes."

We went through the double doors into a large room. It had a high ceiling and three long tables. The atmosphere was alive with the sound of nervous chatter.

A man from the production company showed us to two spare places at one of the tables. There were chairs around the walls for the parents, so our mums went and sat together.

"Here goes!" Mia said, as we unpacked our bags.

I placed my bread in the basket I'd brought, then took my cupcakes out of the tin and arranged them on the plate. I nudged the crystallised flowers until they were perfectly in place – and that was it!

There was nothing to do now except wait.

I checked out the rest of the table. There was an amazing pyramid of profiteroles and next to that a three-tiered pink-and-white birthday cake with a ballerina made from fondant on the top. It must have taken ages.

Other bakes were less impressive – there was a tray of soggy-looking sausage rolls and a huge savoury tart with a gloopy grey filling. There were quite a few plates of cupcakes.

"Look at all the cupcakes," I said to Mia, my heart sinking.

"None of them are as nice as yours," Mia whispered.

"Thanks," I said, but I was starting to feel very nervous. What if the judges thought they were unoriginal? Should I have done something more exciting?

At long last the judges came in. Mum had warned me that the judges from the TV show would be far too busy to attend the local auditions. Instead, we were being judged by three home economists – food experts who worked for the production company. They wore white coats and held clipboards and pens. They each inspected a different table, stopping by contestants and sampling their baking in turn.

The judge at our table was a sensible-looking lady with short grey hair and glasses. She didn't spend long considering the grey pastry tart or the soggy sausage rolls, but she spent ages questioning the boy who'd made the profiteroles and the girl who'd done the ballerina cake. She even got one of the other judges to taste the cake. Finally, it was my turn.

"Hello, Hannah," the lady said, checking

my name badge. "What have you brought with you today?"

"A loaf of *Vollkornbrot*," I said. "And some chocolate and olive oil cupcakes."

"Why *Vollkornbrot*? That's an unusual choice."

"My friend is German and he's been teaching me about German baking," I explained.

"And what else do you know about German baking?" the judge asked.

"Oh, quite a bit now. Stefan – that's my friend – has told me lots. Did you know that there are over a thousand different breads in Germany? They love pastries too, and they like to use a mixture of sugar and spice to flavour them, like Stollen at Christmas—" I broke off, not wanting to talk too much, but the judge looked pleased.

"You clearly have a passion for baking."

I beamed. "It's my favourite thing in the world."

The judge smiled back. "Mine too. Now, let's try some of this bread."

She cut a slice and tasted it. I waited anxiously. "Very good, Hannah," she said. "Well done." I glowed and caught Mia's eye. She gave me a thumbs-up.

Next, the judge cut one of my cupcakes in half. She held it up to inspect the sponge and ganache. Then she took the flower off. "Did you make this yourself or did someone do it for you?"

"I crystallised it myself. It's from our garden."

The judge bit into the cupcake. She finished her mouthful and looked at me. "This is an excellent cupcake," she said. "Quite light for a chocolate cake, but that's offset perfectly by the richness of the ganache. I'd like to get my colleagues to come and have a taste."

Yes! That had to be a good sign, didn't it?

It certainly seemed to be. All the judges made nice comments and the first judge wrote some notes. "Thank you very much, Hannah," she said.

"My pleasure," I said, trying to be as polite as possible.

The judge moved on to chat to Mia. I let out a deep breath. I felt shaky with relief.

To my delight, the judge seemed to like Mia's baking too. She said she enjoyed the grown-up combination of dark chocolate, ginger and macadamia nuts in Mia's brownie, and that the pie showed a very sophisticated palate. Once again, the other judges were called over to try, before they moved on to the next contestant.

"Phew!" I whispered to Mia. "I'm glad that's over."

"It seemed to go well," said Mia.

I held up crossed fingers.

When the judges had finished, they went into a different room to discuss the results.

While we were waiting, some of the other contestants came over to say hi. The girl who had made the ballerina cake seemed nice. Her name was Susie. She told us that the boy next to her, the one who'd done the profiteroles, hadn't been able to answer any of the judge's questions on how he had made them. She thought someone must have helped him.

At last, the judges came back and everyone fell silent. Another man had joined them. "Hello, everyone," he said. "I'm David, the producer of the show. The judges have made their decision. If I read your name out, that means you're on our shortlist and we'd like you to stay for this afternoon. Anyone whose name is not on the list, I'm afraid it's the end of the road for you, but thank you very much for coming today." He cleared his throat and started to read.

My heart was pounding so loudly I almost couldn't hear him.

"James Chang, Susie Patterson ..."

I shot a smile at Susie, the ballerina cake girl. She looked delighted.

"Hannah Hallett."

Me! He'd read out my name! I held my breath, hoping and hoping they'd call out Mia too.

"Mia Evans."

I only just stopped myself whooping out loud. We'd both made it! The other names didn't mean much to me, though I did notice the boy with the profiteroles was out.

"There will now be a half-hour break and then we'd like to interview the people on the shortlist one at a time," said David, the producer. "We'll be filming the interview and we may also ask some of you to demonstrate weighing and mixing ingredients while we chat to you. Emily will come and tell you what order we'd like to see you in, but for now, just relax and have some lunch."

The room erupted into noise. It was easy to spot the people on the shortlist because they were jumping up and down, smiling and laughing. The people who hadn't been picked looked very disappointed as they packed away their things. Soon, the room was much emptier. Only fifteen people had been chosen.

Mia and I sat with our mums to have our packed lunches.

"What do you think they'll ask?" I said.

"Probably similar questions to those they asked on the form," said Mum. "Why you like baking, what you like to bake, that sort of thing."

"They'll want to see how confident you are, and how well you'll come across on the TV," said Mia's mum.

"I don't like the idea of being filmed," said Mia.

"Mia!" I poked her arm. "If you're on the programme, you'll be filmed all the time!"

"Try to relax," her mum said. "Be yourself and forget the cameras are there."

"You'll be fine," Mum said.

I squeezed her hand. "We both will be. You'll see."

TIPS FOR AUDITIONING FOR A BAKING SHOW

· Be polite.
· Be enthusiastic.
· Speak clearly and make eye contact.
· Smile a lot!
· (And, of course, bake something
  delicious!!!!)

9

I was one of the first to go into the interview room. I was glad – it was better than sitting around feeling nervous. I was shown into a room where a table was set up with flour, eggs, butter, sugar, some scales and a mixing bowl, as well as a few cooking utensils. The producer, David, was in there, along with Emily, and a cameraman and a soundman with a big furry microphone on a stick.

"This is a combination of a chat and a screen test," David explained. "A screen test is where we see how well you come across on camera and our chat will give us a chance to get to know you a bit better. Please sit down, relax and try to ignore the camera."

"OK," I said. *This was really exciting!*

"So, Hannah, how long have you been interested in baking?" David asked.

"All my life," I told him. "I've been baking with my mum since I was really little."

David asked me about my mum being a baker. I told him all about moving to Ashingham and how amazing the bakery was and how much I loved learning about new things like German baking.

Within a minute or two I had forgotten all about the camera, and when David asked me if I would stand behind the table to measure out butter and sugar and start creaming them together, I felt really at home.

"And cut!" David said. "That was great, Hannah."

When I got back to the big room, Mia wanted to know all about it. "You were in for ages," she said. There were two people between me and her. They didn't seem to be in for anything like the length of time I was. I didn't know if that was a good or bad thing. Then it was Mia's turn. She was back very quickly.

"Well?" I said. "How did it go?"

"It was horrible!" she wailed. "Everyone listening and looking at me and filming me. I kept forgetting what I was saying." She put her hands over her face. "I'm so glad it's over."

"Um, sweetie," Mia's mum said. "If you really didn't like it, are you sure you want to be on the show?"

"Of course I do!" Mia said. "Well, I want to do the baking and meet the judges and stuff—"

"But there'll be cameras everywhere if you make it through – not just one."

"And there'll be lots of people looking at you," Mum said.

Mia swallowed. "Oh well, I probably haven't got in anyway," she said with a shrug.

As we made our way home, I felt happy and relieved. Mia and I had both done the best we could. It was all down to the judges now.

The days ticked slowly by. No letter from the production company arrived in the post and Mum had no email either. The news that Mia and I had gone for auditions for a TV show had spread around school and everyone kept asking us if we had heard anything. It was horrible having to keep saying no. I just wanted to find out!

I distracted myself by trying to think up

new ways to get Miss Harris and Stefan together. I needed to get them to meet again but I couldn't think how. It wasn't as if I could drag them both to the same place.

I had almost given up when they both came into the bakery one day after school. I was serving Miss Harris when Stefan walked in. I nearly dropped the bag containing Miss Harris's éclair. This was the chance I'd been waiting for!

"Hi, Stefan!" I said, waving madly. "Miss Harris, you remember Stefan, don't you? You met at the workshop."

"Yes, I remember." Miss Harris took the éclair from me. "Thanks, Hannah. I'd better pay Paula."

"No, wait!" I exclaimed as she headed towards the till.

She stopped, looking surprised.

"Um..." I felt my cheeks turn pink. What could I say? *Talk to Stefan, Miss Harris. I bet you'll like each other.* But of course I couldn't – well, not without coming across as a total nutter.

"Um ..." I looked from one to the other. "Stefan likes running!" I said desperately.

Miss Harris gave me a bemused look.

"Yes, yes, I do," Stefan said.

They both looked at me as if expecting me to say something more.

Miss Harris backed away from the counter. "You know, I really had better get going."

She paid and hurried out of the shop as quickly as she could. Mia, who had heard the exchange, gave me a sympathetic look as she served Stefan.

Afterwards, we retreated to the staffroom. "That didn't go well," Mia said.

"I just want them to start talking," I said.

"Maybe they're not suited to each other," Mia said.

"Maybe." I sighed.

That evening, when Mum and I got home, there was an envelope on the kitchen table. It was thick, cream paper, with a London postmark and it was addressed to me. My heart missed a beat. "Do you think this is what I think it is?"

"It looks as though it might be," said Mum excitedly. "Open it, then!"

I took a breath and tore open the envelope.

My fingers were trembling so badly I could hardly get the letter out. What was it going to say?

Dear Hannah,

I am delighted to tell you that you have been selected to appear in the television show, *Junior Brilliant Baker* ...

The words blurred in front of my eyes. I blinked and re-read them. I was in the show! Me! *I* was one of the twelve contestants.

"Mum, I'm in!" I said.

"Oh, my goodness!" said Mum. "Oh, Hannah. Wow! That's wonderful news!"

"I've got to ring Mia," I said.

Mum looked worried. "Just remember, she might not have got in. Be sensitive."

"I will," I promised. I grabbed my phone and pressed Mia's number. My tummy lurched nervously as I waited for her to answer. How should I react if she hadn't got through? I wanted more than anything for us to do it together.

Mia answered. "Hello?"

"Mia! I've just heard from *Junior Brilliant Baker*. Have you?"

"Yeah, I did too." Her voice was flat. "I didn't get in."

The excitement drained out of me. "Oh. Oh no."

"How about you?"

My lips felt very dry. "I, um ... I did."

"You got in?" she asked.

"Uh-huh."

Mia's voice changed. "Hannah, that's amazing! That's awesome! That's incredible!" Her delight was genuine. I could hear it in every word. "You sounded so down, I just assumed you hadn't got in either!"

"You don't mind?"

"No," she said. "Not really. I hated being filmed at that interview. I'm not surprised they didn't ask me, but I'm *so* glad they asked you. I'll be able to help you think of recipes and practise and – OMG! – you're going to be on JBB!"

"I know!" My voice rose.

Mia squealed and I started jumping up and down. I was going to be on JBB! It was the best feeling in the whole world!

I texted Misha, Alice and Lara that night. By the time I got to school the next day it seemed that almost everybody had heard. I was glad Mia had decided she didn't want to be on the show. It would have been really hard if she had been upset, and I was thrilled that she was so pleased for me. She pored over the information the producers had sent. As well as a contract for Mum to fill in, there was a shooting schedule telling me the days

I would be needed – they would be filming during three weeks in July and August at the start of the school holidays, and – the part that interested me and Mia most – a list of the bakes I would be doing if I stayed in the contest right until the final.

In each of the first four rounds, we had to do a Follow-a-Recipe challenge, where the judges would give us a recipe, and after that we had to do a Show-You're-a-Star bake where we baked something of our own from scratch.

My heart leaped when I saw that the first round was bread. That suited me just fine! The second round was sweet pastry. That should be good too. The third was cakes and the fourth was savoury pastry. The production team had decided not to tell us yet what we would have to do if we got into the semi-final and final.

I couldn't wait for it to start!

I was so busy thinking about the filming that the final few weeks of term passed in a flash. I got used to being pointed at and people whispering at school. I didn't mind – I was too excited to care. I spent every free moment baking and reading baking books. What would the other contestants be like? What would we have to bake? What Show-You're-a-Star bakes should I do? I didn't want to bore people so I tried not to talk about it too much – well, except to Mia – but it was really hard. I kept drifting into daydreams and at night my real dreams were filled with the competition. Sometimes I did well but, more often than not, everything went wrong.

My birthday was on Friday, the first of August, which was also the day the second round of the show would be filmed. Mum asked what I wanted to do to celebrate but, for once, I didn't feel like planning anything. Being on the show was going to be enough of a birthday treat. (That was if I even reached the second round! I might be eliminated in the first round.)

However, despite that, Alice, Misha and Lara seemed determined I was going to have a birthday sleepover at the least. On Saturday, the day after we broke up for the summer, Alice rang me.

"Let's have the sleepover at my house the night before your birthday – on Thursday?" Alice said.

"I can't," I said. "I'll have to get up really early on Friday to go to the filming."

"But we can go to bed early and you can ask your mum to pick you up from mine in the morning."

"I'm not sure," I said. "Maybe I could just come over for the evening instead?"

"But we haven't had a sleepover in ages," protested Alice. "It'll be OK. We all want you to do well on the show so we're not going to be stupid and wreck your chances. We'll just have a fun evening – watch a DVD, have some popcorn and then go to bed."

I gave in. It did sound nice. "OK. Let me check with Mum."

I half-expected Mum to say no, but instead

she said, "That's great. It'll do you good to have a break. You always seem to be in the kitchen or have your head in a recipe book these days. It'll be a good distraction the night before – stop you getting too anxious."

"I'll tell Alice yes then," I said. I was pleased. It would be brilliant to see everyone and I knew they would be sensible and let me get some sleep.

Mum nodded. "Have you made a final decision on the bread rolls you're going to bake for the first round yet?"

I'd decided a few weeks ago that I was going to bake bread rolls in the first round, and I had been trying out different flavours and shapes ever since. Mum, Mark and the twins had been eating them most nights.

"I think so," I said. "I'm going to do the rosemary and orange blossom honey round roll and the fennel and thyme knot. I've had an idea for how to display them. Can I show you?"

I fetched my journal and showed Mum the picture I had drawn. "What do you think?"

Hannah's Herb Garden

Mum smiled. "I love it."

"I still need to make sure I get my timings right," I said. "I'm going to work on that tomorrow."

"Then Monday is the big day," said Mum.

I felt my stomach twist. *The big day.* I was starting to feel nervous now. By Monday evening, my JBB dream would either be all over – or I'd be through to the second round. I took a deep breath, and decided to get some extra practice in before dinner.

10

On Monday morning, Mum and I set off at
half past seven. The filming was taking place
in a TV studio just outside London, about an
hour and a half's drive away. Butterflies the
size of seagulls were flapping in my tummy.
I was really glad Mum was coming with me.
She had got up extra early to start the baking
before Dylan took over. Mia was helping
Paula in the shop today and Paula's sister
had also said she would come during the
lunchtime rush.

As I got out of the car in front of the huge
studio, I felt so tense I almost wished we
could get straight back into the car again.
What if I couldn't do the Follow-a-Recipe

challenge? What if my bread rolls went wrong? What if everyone else was better than me?

Emily, the production assistant from the auditions, was in the reception area when we arrived. She greeted us warmly and showed us to a room she called the Green Room. The other contestants were already there, each with an adult. There were five girls and six boys.

I spotted Susie, the other contestant from Nottingham, and felt a rush of relief. At least there was one person I knew. We smiled at each other.

"Hi," she said.

"Hi." I tried to swallow my nerves. "This is so weird, isn't it?"

She nodded. "I'm terrified."

"Me too," I admitted.

Mum overheard us. "Don't worry. I'm sure you'll both be fine when you get started."

David, the producer, came in with a lady called Jenny, who was the director of the show.

"Right, everyone, in a moment you'll go through to the kitchen to prepare for the first challenge," David said. "Parents, wait here and we'll show you to the viewing room. You'll be able to watch what's happening from there."

We all stood up. "Good luck," Mum said.

"Thanks," I said. She kissed my hair and I followed the others out of the room and down a long corridor. It was time to enter the JBB kitchen for the first time!

Apart from the fact that it was filled with cameras and lights, the kitchen looked exactly the same as it does on TV. There were twelve different workstations, all set up with baking equipment. I couldn't see the judges, but I spotted Jamie and Chloe, the two presenters. Chloe's blonde hair was in plaits, Jamie's was dark and spiky, and both of them were wearing bright T-shirts with the JBB logo on.

They came over to us. "Hi, guys!"

It was so weird. I was used to seeing them on the TV and now they were standing here talking to us.

Susie nudged me hard. I followed her gaze and caught my breath. The two JBB judges – Pierre and Sandra – had arrived. Pierre had a wrinkled, tanned face, grey hair and bright blue eyes. Sandra looked a bit older than my mum. She had dark hair cut in a sleek bob and was smiling widely. I stared at them in awe. Mum thinks Pierre is one of the best bakers in the world, and we have all of Sandra's recipe books at home.

"Hello, everyone," said Sandra. "Well, this is the start of it all. Are you nervous?"

We nodded.

"That's completely understandable," she said. "But remember you've all been chosen because you impressed our judges in the auditions. Try to forget the cameras and enjoy the baking."

Pierre nodded. "You are all very young and taking your first steps on the long road to becoming bakers. It's a road *I* have not reached the end of yet, and I am many years older than you. You can learn from everything you bake, whether it turns out well or badly. You must listen to advice from people you respect if you are serious about becoming a good baker. Do you understand?"

I felt a crazy urge to run up to him and say, "I want to be a good baker! I'm going to do everything you say!"

"Right, it's time to get your aprons on," said Jamie.

We were shown to our workstations and given special *Junior Brilliant Baker* aprons. We each had an oven, scales, a mixer and every kind of utensil or bowl we could possibly need. One of the crew came to check that we knew how to work everything. And then it was time for the filming to start and to find out what the challenge was.

Sandra and Pierre stood at the front of the room. "Today, you will be baking one of my favourite snacks," Sandra said. "Grissini, flavoured with sea salt and rosemary."

Grissini. They were breadsticks just like the ones we'd made at Mum's bread-making workshop! I grinned in relief. I was sure I could manage breadsticks.

"You have an hour and a half to make the grissini following my recipe," said Pierre.

"Are you ready to get started, Brilliant Bakers?" Jamie said.

"Yes!" we all shouted.

"Then let the baking … begin!" said Chloe.

I read through Pierre's recipe several times. It was similar to Mum's, but Pierre wanted us to prove the dough for longer. He also wanted us to bake the breadsticks for a much shorter time at a higher temperature. There were no instructions on how to shape the breadsticks, though – it looked as if we had to decide that for ourselves.

Still, there was nothing I felt too worried about.

I glanced round the room. Some of the others were frowning over the recipe, while others had started to measure out the flour and yeast.

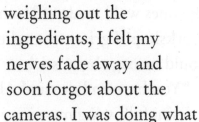

Mum was right. As I began weighing out the ingredients, I felt my nerves fade away and soon forgot about the cameras. I was doing what I loved – baking. Chloe and Jamie walked around the room, stopping at different workstations to chat.

Chloe came up to me just as I was kneading my dough.

"How's it going, Hannah?"

"Good, thanks," I said with a smile. And it was. The dough was a bit sticky at the moment, but it was supposed to be. I still had a lot of kneading to do.

"Have you made grissini before?' Chloe asked.

I nodded and told her about Mum's workshop, then she moved on. I kneaded

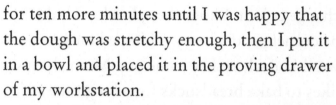

for ten more minutes until I was happy that the dough was stretchy enough, then I put it in a bowl and placed it in the proving drawer of my workstation.

Some of the others had finished too. While we waited for the dough to prove, we chatted. I talked to Susie, Tom, Raj, Issy and Ebony, who all had workstations nearest mine. They were all really nice. I wished Mia had been there too, I knew she'd have liked them – they were as baking-mad as we were!

After half an hour, I went to get my dough. It had doubled in size and was springy to touch. Exactly how it was supposed to be. I shaped and rolled the breadsticks, added the rosemary and sprinkled them with a little sea salt, then put them in the oven.

I watched anxiously through the door as they started to change colour. I knew breadsticks should be crunchy, not chewy – I hoped mine would be when they came out. Mum always likes to bake breadsticks for a long time at a low temperature to make sure they dry out properly, but Pierre's recipe was the opposite. I checked the clock. I had plenty of time. Some of the other contestants, like Ebony, seemed to be quite far behind. She was only just putting her breadsticks in the oven and looked a bit flustered. I wondered if something had gone wrong.

But there wasn't time to worry about anyone else. I had to concentrate on my own bake. Happily, when I took the breadsticks out, I was pleased. They were golden brown, a little bit uneven but not too wonky. I snapped one and it broke with a sharp snap.

The judges always judged the Follow-a-Recipe challenge without knowing who had baked which batch, so we all had to wait in a line while Sandra and Pierre tasted the different breadsticks and said what they thought. Mine were first. Even though I knew they had turned out well, my heart was pounding as the judges each took one from the plate.

Pierre broke one in half. *Snap!* He smiled. "A good start."

"And a nice even bake," said Sandra, inspecting the breadstick she was holding.

They each took a bite and nodded appreciatively as they crunched.

"Very good indeed," said Sandra. "Just the right amount of flavouring and very crisp."

Pierre nodded in agreement. "Whoever made these should be very pleased."

I wanted to jump up and say "It was me!" but we'd been told by Jamie and Chloe that we had to stay as still as possible.

Not everyone was so lucky. Ebony's breadsticks were under-baked, Raj's weren't baked evenly and Tom's were too chewy. Susie had done well, as had a quiet boy called Andrew. At the end of the judging we all held our breath as Pierre and Sandra chatted and then they put the bakes in order from worst to best. They started by asking who had made the breadsticks they thought were the worst – it was Ebony. I felt really sorry for her – she looked as if she wanted to cry.

Sandra and Pierre worked their way up through the bakes. I kept expecting my name to be called out, but it wasn't. As we got to the top three places, I started to feel very excited. Susie had the third-best bake, Andrew had the second-best ...

"And the winner is these breadsticks here," said Sandra. She pointed at a plate of breadsticks. They were MINE!

"Who made them?" asked Pierre.

I stood up. He and Sandra smiled at me, and it was the best feeling ever!

I couldn't wait to get to the Green Room and see Mum. She gave me a massive hug. "Well done, Hannah! I'm so proud of you."

I felt pretty proud of myself, but I knew it was only the start of the competition. There were still several rounds to go and plenty of chances for things to go wrong.

A sandwich lunch was laid out on a big table and I found I was starving. I'd been too nervous to have any breakfast, but I felt much calmer now. I couldn't wait to get started on the next round!

In the afternoon, the second challenge was our Show-You're-a-Star bake, and I felt full of confidence. I had made the bread rolls so many times that I could have made them with my eyes closed. Everything went according to plan: the dough rose nicely and when I shaped the rolls they looked just like I had practised.

By the time we were told to stop, I had twelve rolls – six rosemary and orange blossom honey round rolls, and six fennel and thyme knots. They looked great in their little plant pots. I put the labels on and stood back proudly.

Pierre and Sandra started to go round the benches. It seemed that a few of the others had run into problems – dough hadn't risen, loaves hadn't baked evenly or had been over-baked. The people who had chosen to make unleavened bread had done better – Issy had made pitta bread, which both judges really liked, and Tom had done chapattis. Susie did well again – she'd made focaccia and the judges praised its flavour and texture.

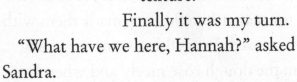

Finally it was my turn.

"What have we here, Hannah?" asked Sandra.

"It's a herb garden," I explained. "The herbs came from my garden at home. I wanted the rolls to be in a plant pot so they look as if they're growing in a garden."

"I like it," said Pierre. "It tells a story."

"And look at this," said Sandra, as she inspected the slate tags. "The attention to detail is super, Hannah. Let's see what they taste like."

To my relief, both judges started to smile as soon as they bit into the rolls. "These are really excellent," said Sandra. "A good bite to the crust, but soft inside."

Pierre nodded. "Maybe next time you could use a touch more rosemary and a little less fennel. The flavour is very strong. But the bake is good overall."

As they moved away, I wanted to collapse in a heap on the floor. I was so relieved.

115

We had a break while the judges went away to make their decision. No one said much. It was very nerve-wracking. Eventually the judges came back and we lined up again.

"You all did really well today," Sandra said warmly. "It's not easy to bake bread within time constraints and in an unfamiliar kitchen, so you should all be proud of yourselves.

"Now, I'd like to announce the winner of the first round. This week our Junior Brilliant Baker is ... Hannah Hallett."

I almost fell off my stool. I knew I'd had a good first bake, but I had hardly dared let myself hope I would be today's winner. "Thank you!" I gasped.

Susie was sitting next to me. "Well done!" she whispered.

"Congratulations, Hannah," said Pierre. "You did very well in both challenges. You obviously have a lot of talent."

"Unfortunately, though, two people must leave us," Sandra went on. "And those people are ..." She paused. Everyone else looked very nervous. "Raj and Ebony."

"The rest of you, we will see you back here on Friday for the sweet pastry round," said Pierre.

Susie and I went to commiserate with Raj and Ebony. They were upset, but Pierre and Sandra gave them both goody bags to take home and posed for pictures and signed autographs, and by the time we got back to the Green Room, they looked happier.

On the way home, I took my phone out of Mum's bag. It was full of messages from Mia, Misha, Alice, Lara, Dylan, Mark and George.

I replied to them all with a joint text saying that I'd got through and had been crowned Junior Brilliant Baker for this week. I'd text them separately later.

"I'm exhausted," I said, flopping back in my seat.

Mum smiled. "I'm not surprised. And in

a few days' time you've got to do it all over again!"

I nodded and took my journal out of her bag. She was right. There was no time to rest. I had to start thinking about the second round!

11

"Strawberry tart? Raspberry and custard?" Mia said to me the next day. She'd come round first thing and all we'd talked about was *Junior Brilliant Baker*. After I'd told her every little detail about the filming, we started trying to decide what I should bake for the next challenge. It was sweet pastry and I wanted to make a tart. The trouble was choosing what type. It needed to be impressive, but not too complicated in case it went wrong on the day.

"Maybe I should I do something simple and classic, like a lemon tart," I said.

"You could, but if it doesn't turn out well you won't have any room to hide," said Mia.

"Sandra makes an amazing lemon tart – it's like her signature dish. It would be hard to compete with that, even if yours was perfect."

It was a good point. "How about something more inventive, then?"

"What about a twist on a classic? Say, a Black Forest gateau, but as a tart, or a Bakewell with fresh raspberries?" Mia suggested.

I liked that idea. "Let's make a list." I opened my journal. "How about a toffee apple tart?"

"That sounds yummy. Or a millionaires' shortbread tart?"

By the time we'd finished we had a whole page of possibilities. "How am I ever going to decide?" I said.

Mia grinned. "Easy. Just bake them all and see which you like best!"

TART IDEAS

Black Forest gateau

Bakewell with fresh raspberries

 Toffee apple

Millionaires' shortbread

Pear and almond

Raspberry and dark chocolate

Strawberry and custard

When Mia went home, I stayed in my room, poring over Mum's recipe books and searching on the Internet. I would make up my own recipe in the end but I wanted to look at other people's too. You can get really good ideas and hints and tips that way. I printed off pages and made lots of notes.

I didn't eat lunch. Instead, I carefully sorted the recipes into piles – one pile of recipes that had ideas I liked and wanted to try out, one of recipes that had interesting tips in, and one pile of definite Nos. Soon I was surrounded by papers and books. Whenever I thought I could stop, I would find another link to an interesting recipe that I wanted to print out. It had started off being fun, but now I had far too many ideas and my head was beginning to ache. How was I ever going to make sense of it all?

I was
surveying
the piles
and
wondering
what to do when
the door burst open and
Molly came running into my room. "Ella's chasing me, Hannah!" she shrieked. "Can I hide in here ... whoa!"

She skidded on books and papers and fell over, mixing the piles of recipes together as she fell. "Molly!" I yelled.

"Sorry." Molly scrambled to her feet.

At that moment, Ella came running in. "Found you!" she cried, skidding on a cookery book and breaking its spine. "Whoops, sorry, Hannah!"

Anger rushed through me. I hardly ever lose my temper, but I'd worked hard all afternoon and they'd ruined it. "Get out, both of you!" I shouted. "Get out right now! NOW!"

The twins looked at each other in alarm, then turned and ran. I heard Molly burst into tears.

Guilt pricked at me and that made me feel worse.

I slammed my bedroom door shut and began sorting through the piles. I was tired, I didn't know what recipe I was going to do, and I was horribly aware that I only had two days left to work it out.

By early evening I had finally worked out
a shortlist – toffee apple; dark chocolate
and fresh raspberries; and strawberry and
custard. I had written out recipes for all of
them and Mark had taken
me shopping so I could try
them out. I was melting
some chocolate for the
chocolate and raspberry tart when
Mum got home.

"Stefan's coming for dinner," she told me.
"I'm going to make a spaghetti bolognese.
What are you baking?"

I explained about the tarts. Mum liked all
my ideas. "How about we taste them tonight
and help you choose which one?"

"Yes please!" I said.

She set to work on dinner while I finished
the chocolate filling and then poured it over
the raspberries I had arranged in the pastry
case I had baked earlier.

"I've been thinking about your birthday on Friday," Mum said. "Do you want to do something when we get back?"

"I don't know." I remembered how tired I had been the night before. "I think I'll just want to go to bed."

"Are you sure?" Mum asked. "We could go out for a meal?"

I shook my head.

"OK. Well, maybe we can do something later whenever you finish the filming," said Mum.

My heart gave a little flip. It was weird to imagine the filming for JBB being over. The competition was beginning to take over my life.

When Stefan arrived, he joined us in the kitchen. When I told him that the next round was sweet pastry, he talked about a special German shortcrust pastry called *Mürbeteig*. It's a pastry that doesn't have any egg in it and is more crumbly than traditional shortcrust pastry. I wondered if I should try making it for the competition. German bread had worked in the auditions; maybe German pastry would help in the pastry round too.

After dinner, everyone tried my tarts. The strawberry and custard tart and the toffee apple tart were both yummy, but we all agreed that the dark chocolate tart with raspberries was by far the best. I still wanted to tweak the recipe a bit – to try it out with the German pastry and get the filling smoother and even richer. I also thought maybe I should add another flavour to it, but I couldn't decide what.

I fell into bed that night feeling completely exhausted. I'd planned to spend the whole of the next day baking, but Mum had said she didn't want me on my own for too long, so I would go into the bakery in the morning. Luckily, Mark was working at home in the afternoon, which meant I'd be able to go home and practise then.

Next day, for the first time ever, I found myself itching to leave the bakery. I kept thinking of little changes to make to my recipe, and I was so busy making notes that I didn't help out as much as I usually did.

At last Mark came to pick me up, and when we got home, I headed straight for the kitchen. Unfortunately, my experiment with German pastry didn't go well. I just couldn't seem to get the dough to hold together and the tart just leaked or crumbled.

At around half past four, Mark popped his head into the kitchen. "I'm going to pick up the twins. I thought I might take them for a pizza. Do you want to come?"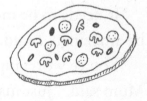

I shook my head. "I can't. I need to get this tart right."

"Well, best that I keep the girls out of your way then," he said. "Your mum will be back soon – she's just texted to say she's leaving the bakery. Maybe she can help you with it?"

"Mmm," I said. I didn't want Mum's help, though. It would sort of feel like cheating and I wanted to do it on my own.

By the time Mum arrived, I was staring at a ball of pastry dough which was crumbling to pieces on the table in front of me. "Oh, this is just not working!" I said.

"What are you doing?" Mum asked.

I told her about the German pastry.

"But the pastry you made last night was fine," Mum said.

"It needs to be more than fine. It needs to be amazing," I said.

"You're worrying too much, sweetheart," Mum said. "Just make pastry like you always do and you won't have a problem. You did really well in the first round." She looked at the flour-spattered kitchen. "Now, I think you've done enough baking for today. Let's clear up."

She started moving bowls over to the sink and I felt frustration swell inside me. She didn't understand. I'd loved winning the first round and I wanted to do it again – or at least be one of the best. And if that meant practising every single second and tweaking my recipe over and over again until the last possible minute, that's what I would do.

Mum caught the expression on my face. "Come on, Hannah," she said, her tone softening. "You're getting yourself stressed out about this for no reason. Don't try and change things that don't need changing."

"You mean just be boring," I said.

Mum fixed me with a look. "That's not what I said. You're practising too much, getting too stressed, that's all."

I stamped my foot. "That's because I have to. Why don't you get it?"

Mum frowned. "Hannah, I'm only trying to help."

"Well, don't!"

"That's it!" Mum snapped. "Out of the kitchen right now, young lady. I've had enough of this attitude."

I lost my temper too. "I just want it to be

perfect! What's wrong with that?" I stomped up the stairs, slamming my bedroom door.

Mum waited for me to calm down, then made me apologise and clean up the kitchen on my own.

Afterwards, I rang Mia. "She's just trying to help," Mia said when I told her about it.

"Well, I wish she would try and be a bit more understanding," I said.

"I know," Mia said. "I know I'd be feeling really stressed if I were you. Is your mum going to be able to go with you on Friday to the filming?"

"Yes. Miss Harris has volunteered to help Dylan in the kitchen, because Fridays are usually busy. She told Mum she'd enjoy it. Are you coming to the bakery tomorrow?"

"Yes, what about you?"

"Yes, Mum says I have to because Mark's at his office all day. I'm going to come home as soon as she lets me though and start practising then. I'll get this tart right, even if it means staying up all night!"

"Um, Hannah ... you can't practise

tomorrow night. It's your birthday sleepover, remember?" Mia said.

I'd completely forgotten. "Oh no! I have to practise! I can't go to a sleepover tomorrow."

"Oh." Mia hesitated. "But everyone's really looking forward to it."

Guilt twisted my insides. What should I do? It was lovely that my friends wanted to celebrate my birthday, but I just had too much to do.

Mia broke the silence. "Look, don't worry. You know we all just want you to do well in the competition. If you have to practise, then we'll just have the sleepover another time. The others will understand."

"Maybe next week?" I said in relief.

"Lara's on holiday next week," Mia reminded me. "But perhaps after that?"

"I'm sorry," I said. "I'll phone Alice and the others and tell them. Or" – an idea struck me – "you could have the sleepover anyway, just without me."

"It's supposed to be for your birthday,

Hannah," said Mia. "We don't want to do it without you."

I was glad Mia had said that, but it made me feel even more guilty.

The phone calls weren't fun to make. Alice, Misha and Lara had been busy at the riding stables they went to all week and we hadn't seen each other since school broke up. They tried to sound OK about me cancelling but I could tell they were disappointed.

"We've got to do *something* for your birthday," said Misha. "How about we at least go to Harry's for an ice cream tomorrow morning?"

Harry's is a fab ice-cream parlour in town. Going for an ice cream sounded nice. It also wouldn't take up much time – and it was time I'd be at the bakery anyway. "OK," I said.

"Brilliant. I'll tell the others," Misha said. "And no cancelling that!"

"I won't," I promised.

Mia and I walked to Harry's together the next morning. Just before we left, I had a brainwave. I'd been thinking about the extra flavour for my tart and now I had it – fresh mint would be delicious added to the dark chocolate. I could decorate it with crystallised mint leaves. I told Mia and she thought it sounded like a great idea. I couldn't wait to get home to try it out.

When we got to Harry's, the others were already there. They wanted to know all about the competition. But they're definitely not as baking-mad as Mia and I are, so after about twenty minutes, I could see they were losing interest. They started gossiping about people

from school and messing around, making hats out of the paper napkins. I usually love joining in with things like that, but today I was too distracted. It was as if my body was with my friends and my mind was back in the kitchen.

"Hannah, why do you keep looking at your watch?" Misha asked me suddenly.

I jumped guiltily. "Sorry."

"She's probably just trying to work out how long she has to stay and eat ice cream before she can get back to baking," teased Alice.

I shifted uncomfortably in my chair, knowing how close to the truth she was.

"Well, don't let us keep you," said Lara, rolling her eyes. "You can go if you want."

"No, no, I'm happy here," I lied. But as the conversation moved on to other things, I found my eyes drifting to my watch again.

"Hannah?" Alice said.

"What?" I realised they were all looking at me.

"Earth to Hannah! Do you want another ice cream?" said Misha.

"Have you been listening to a word we've been saying?" asked Alice.

"Of course!" I said.

They exchanged looks.

"Well, do you want one?" said Misha.

"Um, I'm not sure. I should probably go," I said. I just wasn't enjoying myself. I had too much on my mind.

"Well, I'm staying," said Alice.

"Me too," said Lara.

Mia nodded. "I think I'll have another ice cream too."

"Oh. OK." I wasn't really surprised. I knew I wasn't being very good company at the moment. "Well, I'll see you all later."

They waved me off. As I left Harry's, glancing back in through the window, I saw my friends laughing and joking together and felt a pang of loneliness.

There would be other times at Harry's,

I reassured myself. For now, I had the competition to think about. I turned away and hurried down the street towards the bakery.

12

Mum and I set off early on Friday morning. I'd lost count of the number of times I'd made my tart. I'd decided not to use the German pastry in the end but I hoped that, with the addition of the mint, the tart would give me a chance at getting through to the next round. I felt really anxious and I hadn't slept much. Every time I drifted off I'd ended up having horrible dreams – ingredients suddenly vanishing, tarts burning, people shouting at me, time running out.

Mia, Alice, Misha and Lara had all sent birthday texts and good-luck messages, which was nice but also made me feel guilty about the way I'd behaved at Harry's. I knew

I was being a terrible friend at the moment.

I took a breath. If only I could think straight. My head felt as if it was full of soggy pastry. Oh please, don't let MY pastry be soggy today, I prayed.

"Today, contestants, for the Follow-a-Recipe challenge, we would like you to make us a lemon meringue pie," Sandra told us.

I felt a rush of relief. That was good. I've made lemon meringue pies before, and we had a recipe to follow. What could go wrong? It was just pastry, lemon filling and meringue – as long as I thought about them all separately and stayed calm, I was sure I could do a good job.

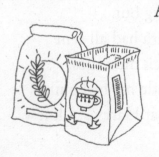

As I was weighing the ingredients for the pastry case, the presenters, Chloe and Jamie, came over.

"How are you feeling today, Hannah?" Chloe asked brightly.

"Good, thanks." I smiled, although I didn't really feel like talking. I just wanted to get on with making my pie.

"You had a great first round," said Jamie. "And you received lots of praise from our judges. Do you think you'll impress them again today?"

"I hope so," I said. He was making me feel even more nervous – everyone clearly expected me to be brilliant, and that was scary.

Chloe smiled. "Good luck!" They moved on to talk to Susie, who was at the workstation next to me.

I weighed and then re-weighed the flour and butter, and started rubbing it together to make a breadcrumb-like texture. When I finally had a ball of dough, I started to roll it out.

It was soon the right size to line the tin, but it looked a little thin so I gathered it into a ball and rolled it out again. Then, as I picked it up, I realised I hadn't rolled it out perfectly evenly so had to start again. It took four attempts before I was happy. As I lifted the pastry gently into the tin, I glanced round. Everyone else had finished their pastry cases and was already starting their lemon filling. Panic gripped me. I was way behind!

I looked at the clock. The pastry case still needed to chill before being blind-baked. And I also had to make the lemon filling and the meringue. If I didn't speed up, I'd be in trouble. I pressed the pastry quickly into the tin, tearing it slightly. I quickly squished the torn edges together, then shoved it into the fridge under the counter.

Chloe came back. "All OK, Hannah? You look a little behind the others."

"I'm fine," I said. I could feel sweat prickling my back. I wished she'd go away.

"Are you worried about whether you'll

finish in time?" Chloe went on. "This is a test where timing is going to be crucial. There's a lot to do."

"I know, but hopefully it'll be fine," I said. Chloe continued to chat as I weighed cornflour and juiced and zested lemons. It was really hard to talk and work at the same time. I felt myself getting more and more flustered. How long should I leave the pastry case in the fridge for? It had to bake for about

141

twenty minutes and then cool before I added the filling and meringue and put it in the oven one last time. *Oh no – the oven! I hadn't preheated it!*

"What's the matter?" Chloe asked.

"The oven! It's not preheating!" I quickly turned the oven on. I was beginning to feel as if I was in one of my nightmares.

To my relief, Chloe left me to it. But my problems didn't stop there. When I took the pastry case out of the fridge I realised I hadn't covered it with cling film – the pastry would be tough now. I couldn't believe I'd forgotten something so simple.

Things went from bad to worse. I overcooked my lemon mixture, then trimmed the pastry case back too far, forgetting that it would shrink while it was baking. When I took my pastry out of the oven, it had cracked at the bottom and it was too small, but there was nothing I could do. The minutes were passing like seconds. I spooned on the lemon filling and added the meringue mixture on top. There was no time to make it pretty. I shoved it in the oven and shut the door with a horrible sick feeling in my stomach. It was going to be a disaster. There were only ten minutes left and the pie needed at least fifteen to cook properly.

With five minutes to go, everyone else was taking their pies out of the oven and arranging them on plates. Some of them looked amazing, with neat pastry cases and golden peaks of meringue.

When I finally took out my pie, I felt like turning and running away. The meringue was very gloopy and, as I tried to prise the pie out of the tin and onto the plate, the pastry cracked and the whole thing fell apart in a big splodge. It was a complete and utter disaster.

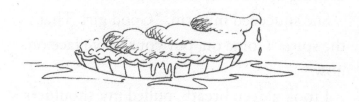

I swallowed hard and looked at the floor. I didn't want to cry on camera.

Chloe must have noticed how upset I was because, as everyone else talked excitedly and took their plates up to the front bench to be judged, she waved the cameras away and came to give me a hug. "Oh, Hannah, don't be upset," she said.

"But it's awful," I whispered, staring at my collapsed pie. A tear rolled down my cheek.

"Everyone has bad days," she said. "It's not the end of the world. You've still got this afternoon to prove yourself. Remember what Pierre said: if you make a mistake, you learn from it and move on."

I managed a small smile. "I think I'll be doing a lot of learning from today," I said, looking at my lemon meringue mess.

She squeezed my arm. "Good girl. That's the spirit. Come on, put your brave face on now."

I took a deep breath, pulled my shoulders back and nodded. I knew I was going to be criticised by the judges, but I was going to be grown up about it. Chloe was right; there was still the afternoon to come. I picked up my plate and carried it to the front.

When it came to it, the judges weren't as horrible as they could have been. "The lemon filling has got just the right amount of sugar in," said Sandra. "And with a bit more cooking the meringue would have crisped up."

"But the pastry ..." Pierre shook his head in disappointment. "No. Just no."

I blushed and looked at the floor. I knew the cameras would be filming me and I wanted to disappear.

No one had had anything like as big a disaster as I had, and my pie was pronounced the worst. Susie's was the best.

"I'm sorry," she said to me as we were sent back to the Green Room for lunch.

"Don't be. It's my own fault. You deserved to win. I'm glad you did," I told her.

She gave me a grateful smile. "Thanks. I bet you'll do brilliantly this afternoon."

"I hope so," I sighed.

TIPS FOR MAKING GOOD MERINGUE

- Be careful not to get any egg yolk in your egg whites.
- Always bring the eggs to room temperature before use - this will help make your meringue fluffier.
- Add the sugar slowly or it will knock the air out of the egg white and your meringue will be heavy.

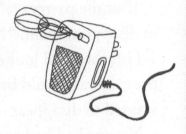

- Don't panic!

Mum gave me a big hug when she saw me. "Oh, Hannah," she said. "Not your finest moment."

"No," I said. "I don't think that will make it to the highlights of the programme – at least, not in a good way."

"What went wrong?" she said.

"I don't know. I just got in a panic."

"Well, try and keep calm this afternoon,"

146

Mum said. "You make fantastic pastry. This should be one of your strongest weeks. Just trust your instincts."

I nodded. I was going to have to do my very best to redeem myself this afternoon if I wanted to stay in the competition.

As I stood looking at the ingredients for my chocolate, mint and raspberry tart, waiting to be told we could start, I felt nerves dancing through every part of my body. I wanted to push the lemon meringue disaster out of my mind, but somehow I couldn't. I felt it hovering over me. *Just one more mistake and I might be out.*

"OK, it's time. Good luck, contestants!" said Chloe.

Jamie took over. "Are you ready? Let the baking ... BEGIN!"

I continued to stare at the ingredients in front of me. Flour, caster sugar, icing sugar, butter.

I'd made pastry hundreds of times, but my mind was completely blank. It didn't help that one of the cameras was filming me. I knew it was because of what had happened this morning – they wanted to see if I'd mess up again.

Just snap out of it, I told myself. I took a deep breath and weighed out the flour and butter then rubbed them together. I ran over everything else I needed to do. I pictured the different steps: making the pastry case, baking it, chopping the chocolate and making the filling.

I glanced down and realised I'd been rubbing the butter and sugar for too long. My hands were warm because I was so nervous, and now, instead of a fine breadcrumb-like mixture, I had a yellow lumpy mess. I wracked my brains. I knew there was something I was supposed to do to solve the problem, but I couldn't remember what. I didn't have time to start again. I'd have to press on.

I added the milk, but too much went in at once – the mixture went slimy and I had to add more flour. I pushed and kneaded and worked the dough frantically. All the rules I knew about making pastry – adding liquid gradually, handling the pastry dough as little as possible, not overworking it – seemed to vanish from my mind. It was as though I'd been taken over by someone else, and that someone had definitely never baked before!

By the time I finally put my tart in the oven, my workstation was in complete chaos. There were dirty bowls, flour and utensils everywhere. Pierre came over at one point and made a disapproving comment. I wasn't surprised. I knew Mum wouldn't have been happy if I'd worked in such a mess at home.

As I cleared up, my heart felt heavy in my chest. My tart wasn't going to be anywhere near as good as I'd hoped.

The only positive thing was that I had plenty of time to decorate it, because I'd been so quick to get it into the oven. I added the fresh raspberries and crystallised mint leaves. It looked nice. The chocolate was dark, rich and smooth and the colour of the raspberries and mint leaves was a pretty contrast. But looking good wouldn't mean a thing if it didn't taste good too.

"Well, this looks really lovely," Sandra said, as she and Pierre arrived at my workstation.

"Excellent presentation, Hannah," said Pierre.

I forced a smile and watched closely as Sandra cut a slice. I could tell the pastry was tough from the way she struggled to get through it with her knife. She slid a slice out and prodded the pastry with the tip of her knife. "The pastry's thin enough, but it looks heavy."

Pierre looked at me. "I noticed you seemed to spend quite a lot of time bringing the pastry together."

"Yes," I said in a small voice. "I overworked it. I'm sorry."

"Well, let's have a taste," said Sandra. She and Pierre both took a forkful. They chewed slowly.

"It's a lovely filling," Sandra said kindly. "Chocolate, mint and raspberry. That's a delicious combination."

Pierre shook his head. "But the pastry … it's not great, Hannah."

I swallowed hard. "I know. I made too many mistakes. It should have been better."

He nodded at me, and they moved on. I stared down at the bench and felt hot tears prickle my eyes.

- Keep everything cold - make sure the butter is cold, use ice-cold liquid and run your hands under a cold tap before working with the dough.

- Add liquid gradually. You might not need it all, and if the pastry is too wet it will be heavy.

- Handle the dough as little as possible - overworked pastry will be tough and chewy.

- Always rest the dough in the fridge before rolling it out. Put cling film over the bowl to stop it becoming tough.

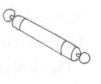

- Brush the top of a pie, pastry or tart with a little beaten egg before it goes in the oven to give it a lovely golden colour.

13

After the judges had gone off to discuss the
results, I lined up with the others to hear
their decision. Sandra told us all how well we
had done and announced that Susie was the
winner of the second round – she had baked a
pineapple, mango and coconut tart that Pierre
and Sandra had described as 'near perfect'.
I was pleased for her but dreaded what was
coming next. Pierre cleared his throat.

Near
Perfect

"The two contestants leaving us today are ..." he said. "Hannah Hallett and Tom Parks."

It was like being hit in the stomach. I felt my shoulders slump. Even though I had done badly in both sections of this round, a part of me had hoped that by some miracle I might still get through to the third round.

"I'm so sorry, Hannah," said Sandra, coming over, followed by a cameraman. "You did really well to get this far. Are you OK?"

"Cross with myself," I said, willing myself not to cry. I swallowed and met her eyes. "But I deserve to go. I didn't do well enough. Everyone else was better than me."

"You will carry on baking, though, won't you?" said Sandra.

"Oh yes," I told her. "Nothing will stop me baking."

She smiled. "Good. I'm sure you have a great future. Good luck."

Pierre came and shook my hand. "Sandra is right. Just remember what I said ..." His blue eyes fixed on mine. "Learn from every mistake. You have a lot of talent, Hannah. I think you will be a great baker one day."

There was a lump in my throat but I swallowed hard. "Thank you, and thank you for having me on the show."

"It's been a pleasure," said Sandra. "Now, go to the Green Room. I'm sure your mum will want to see you."

The others had all gone, but Susie had waited for me. "Bad luck," she said.

"It's fine," I said. "Well done on being the star baker this week." I tried to smile, even though I just wanted to hide away. It wasn't only the competition. I felt guilty about how horrible I'd been to everyone all week. I'd argued with Mum and snapped at the twins and cancelled the sleepover my friends had tried to arrange for my birthday. And I'd barely said a word at the ice-cream date they'd organised instead. I'd messed up big time.

When we walked into the Green Room, Mum gathered me into the biggest ever hug.

"Oh, Hannah. It really wasn't your day," she said.

Suddenly I couldn't hold back my unhappiness any longer. "I'm sorry," I sobbed.

She kissed my head. "Sweetie, you have nothing to be sorry about. Nothing at all. I'm so proud of you for getting this far. You did some brilliant baking in the first round and I know you can make perfect pastry – *you* know you can make pastry. It was just a bad day." Her arms tightened around me.

I felt a bit better. "Thank you," I managed to say. "It's not just the pastry, though. I'm sorry about everything this week."

"Well, you have been a bit difficult," she said, pulling back and looking me in the eyes. "But I know it was only because you cared so much about the competition, so I forgive you."

"What about everyone else? Do you think they'll forgive me too?" I asked. I felt sick when I thought again about how I'd behaved. "I don't think I want to go home!" I gulped.

"Oh, I think you do." Mum took out her smartphone and made a quick call using FaceTime. I heard Paula answer.

"Hi," said Mum. "Did you get my message earlier?"

"Yes. Did it go as you feared?" Paula said. I could hear voices in the background.

"It did. Hannah's out of the competition. Can I show her what you're doing?"

"Put her on!" Paula said.

I took the phone from Mum and saw Paula standing in the bakery. Behind her were Miss Harris, Dylan and Mia. They were peering over her shoulder and waving. I blinked as I realised Stefan was there too.

"Hi, Hannah!" said Paula. "So sorry to hear it didn't go well. Particularly on your birthday. We all think you're amazing, so we're preparing a Well-Done-for-Trying-and-Happy-Birthday party for when you get back."

I felt tears spring to my eyes again. "You're doing that for me?"

"Absolutely! We're so proud of you!"

"Misha, Alice and Lara are coming too," Mia put in. "And Mark and the twins."

"I thought I might bake a lemon meringue pie, Skippy!" said Dylan, grinning wickedly. "Especially for you!"

Despite everything, I chuckled.

Mum took the phone off me. "All right. See you soon, everyone!"

"Bye!" they chorused.

She ended the call. "So, do you think you're forgiven?"

The lump was back in my throat and I nodded. My friends and family were brilliant. I'd been horrible and selfish but they'd forgiven me and they were even planning a party for me. I wanted to get home and say sorry properly. Mum put her arm round my shoulders. "Come on, sweetheart, let's go."

The bakery was packed with people when we arrived – Paula, Dylan and Mia, Miss Harris and Stefan (who, to my surprise, seemed to be laughing and smiling together), Misha, Alice and Lara, and George and his mum, Sarah. And then, of course, there were Mark, Ella and Molly. Ella and Molly squealed and threw themselves at me as I came through the door. I hugged them both tightly.

Mark gave me a bear hug. "You did so well to get as far as you did," he said.

"Thanks." I smiled. Now I'd had the car journey to think about it, I was beginning to realise that there was some truth in what everyone was saying. Over four thousand people had applied to be on *Junior Brilliant Baker* and I'd got down to the final ten. That wasn't bad. "I'm sorry I've been so horrible this week."

Mark squeezed my arm. "Apology accepted. Consider it forgotten."

Mia, Alice, Lara and Misha bounced over. "Happy birthday!" they cried.

"What was it like? What happened?" Misha demanded.

"Your mum said you had a disaster with a lemon meringue pie," said Mia.

"A disaster to end all disasters," I said, rolling my eyes. "But at least I went out with a bang."

Alice hugged me. "Never mind, we still think you're brilliant."

I hugged her back and then the words just rushed out of me. "I'm so, so sorry, everyone. I've been awful, talking about the show all the time and cancelling the sleepover and being no fun at Harry's. I've been a useless friend. I bet you all just want to dump me."

Misha frowned. "Stop with the crazy talk. No one's dumping anyone. You were busy filming a TV show – I mean, how awesome is that?"

"Not so awesome that I had an excuse to be a completely rubbish friend," I said.

"Well, we forgive you your rubbishness,"

said Alice. "And we still, very definitely, want to be your friends."

I felt the guilt that had been turning my stomach in knots start to release its grip. "Thanks," I mumbled. Worried I was going to get tearful again, I reached into the goody bag that the producers had given me. I'd asked Sandra and Pierre to sign photos for all my friends, and Jamie and Chloe had given me some signed photos too. There were also some JBB postcards and signed coasters with the JBB logo on. "Here, these are for all of you," I said.

"Cool!" said Lara. "Thanks."

"Sandra and Pierre's autographs," said Mia, her eyes glowing. "Oh, wow!"

"Well, I, for one, am glad you're not in the competition any more!" said Misha.

"You are?" I said.

"Yes – it means we can rearrange your birthday sleepover!"

"Misha!" Alice said. But I didn't mind. Misha was just

being Misha. I realised then how much I'd missed my friends.

Misha looked at me teasingly. "Come on, Hannah, you know you'd MUCH rather be having fun with us than be on TV."

"Yes," I said, linking her arm and grinning. "You're right."

Miss Harris came over with Stefan. Misha, Alice and Lara said hi and then went to talk to George. I could tell they thought it was strange to be around a teacher out of school hours.

"Well done, Hannah," said Miss Harris. "Disasters happen to us all, and the important thing to remember is that you're a talented baker most of the time. Don't let one bad day make you forget that."

"You should have done the German pastry," said Stefan, giving me a wink. "That would have saved you."

"I don't think anything would have saved me today," I told him. "Particularly not German pastry, the way I was making it. You'll have to show me how to do it one day because each time I tried it was a disaster."

"Any time," he said.

Miss Harris smiled at him. "Stefan's been telling me how much he loves to bake. We were talking about having a German week in Baking Club next term. Maybe he could show us all then."

"I would love to," Stefan said.

I couldn't believe they were getting on so well! I pulled Mia to one side. "OK, what's going on?" I hissed, nodding at Miss Harris and Stefan, who were now talking together in a corner – and standing very close to one another too.

"It's all because of the bakery," said Mia. "You know Miss Harris was here helping today?"

"Yes."

"Well, there was a big rush at lunchtime. Stefan had popped in and he offered to stay and help. That was it. They started talking and seemed to get on really well."

"To think I tried so hard to get them together and it didn't work. I should have just left them in a kitchen on their own!" I said.

Mia nodded. "It's like dough proving. If you leave it in a warm place, the magic just happens."

I realised she was right. Sometimes in life, like in baking, you need to work hard to make things happen, to mix and stir, but at other times you need to put the ingredients together and just step back. I guess the trick is knowing when to put the work in and when to leave things alone.

I looked at Mia, who was smiling as she watched Stefan and Miss Harris. "Thanks," I said suddenly.

164

"What for?"

"For being my best friend."

Mia beamed.

"Time to dance, everyone!" Dylan called, putting some music on.

Misha ran over. "Come on, you two!"

She pulled us into the middle of the bakery shop floor. Alice, George and Lara joined us and Paula started showing off her belly-dancing moves, trying to get Miss Harris and Stefan to join her. Mum and Mark stood with their arms round each other while Dylan showed off some robotic dancing and the twins ran round in mad circles.

I felt a surge of happiness. OK, so I'd been knocked out of *Junior Brilliant Baker* and baked a truly disastrous lemon meringue pie on TV, but I'd also got further than lots of other people, and I'd been the best baker in the first week. I had amazing friends and a wonderful family and my mum owned the best bakery in the world.

Stefan danced over to me. "How are you feeling, Hannah?"

"Good, thanks," I said.

"Just good?" he asked.

I hesitated, then grinned. "No, not just good. I feel A-MA-ZING!"

A cake won't bake itself, but some bakes need a light touch to get the best results!

**Catch up with Hannah and her
best friends in . . .**

When I told my mum she should follow
her dreams and open her own bakery, I didn't
realise it would mean us moving house, leaving
all my friends and starting a new school in
the middle of Year Seven. But that's
exactly what happened.

Can Hannah discover the recipes for friendship,
happiness and the perfect cupcake?